Lion Outwitted by Hare
and Other African Tales

LION OUTWITTED BY HARE
and Other African Tales

Phyllis Savory

Illustrated by Franz Altschuler

Albert Whitman & Company, Chicago

ISBN 0-8075-4556-2
Library of Congress Catalog Card Number 74-126432
Copyright © 1961, 1962, 1963, 1966 by Phyllis Savory
Copyright © 1971 in selection and arrangement
by Albert Whitman & Company
Illustrations Copyright © 1971 by Albert Whitman & Company
All rights reserved, including the right to reproduce
this book or portions thereof in any form.
Published simultaneously in Canada by
George J. McLeod, Limited, Toronto
Printed in the United States of America

Contents

A Note About These Bantu Tales

ABOUT SIXTY YEARS AGO, A LITTLE GIRL GREW UP ON an African farm in Rhodesia. She heard Bantu folktales told to illustrate a point or teach a lesson just as generation after generation of African children had.

Phyllis Savory's early interest in Bantu tales continued into her adult life. She collected stories from many sources, always trying to retain the original flavor and style in her translations. This present selection from four of Phyllis Savory's books includes animal stories reminiscent of folklore from many lands as well as longer narratives filled with magic and romance. A few tales are similar to European favorites, but the added African elements give them a special touch.

While listeners to such tales by the fireside were supposed to profit by the moral, it is a good guess they responded more exuberantly to the heroism and cleverness that provide suspense and humor.

The word "Bantu" is widely used to identify Africans speaking related languages and living in the southern portion of the African continent. The word itself means "person" and was first used to designate certain languages by a German scholar in 1856.

Although language students of today prefer terms other than Bantu, the phrase "Bantu-speaking" is still used for Africans of different tribes who share some common history as evidenced by the similarities of their languages.

The Bantu stories told here are grouped by origin as the author published them. Because tribal names vary in spelling, a note about origins follows.

The first stories are from the Matabele people, also known as the Ndebele, who speak a Zulu dialect. Some of the Matabele people fled north in 1838 to what is now Rhodesia to escape a powerful and harsh Zulu king.

The second group of stories come from Kenya and Malawi. The Agikuyu tribe, also called the Kikuyu, settled in Kenya, probably before the sixteenth century. Other Bantu-speaking tribes on their great migration from the north continued on their way, but the Agikuyu were content with their beautiful new homeland. By contrast, the tellers of the other tales in this section are from the Angoni tribe, also known as Ngoni, a group who, like the Matabele, returned northward to escape the Zulu unrest.

The Zulu stories in the third section are from the South African province of Natal, not far from Swaziland. The Zulu people are believed to have arrived here after a migration of centuries that covered thousands of miles. In the seventeenth century they settled in what is still known as Zululand.

Finally come the Xhosa fireside tales. The Xhosa tribe, also called Xosa and pronounced "kosa," were never conquered by the Zulus. They live in the southernmost province of South Africa, the Cape of Good Hope.

Tales Told by the Matabele People

How the Lion Was
Outwitted by the Hare

AN ANGRY FIRE WAS RAGING ACROSS THE PLAINS
near the Zambezi River and already it had bitten far
into the forest lands next to the open portion.

The tinder dry grass in many places was taller
than the height of a man. Mighty was the racing
demon of fire that ate up the grass for miles on either
side.

The high wind drove the flames along. All living
creatures were straining every limb to keep beyond
the heat.

Elephant, lion, leopard, giraffe, cheetah—all
wild things ran together in a race to save their lives.
With the danger of fire close, the animals showed no

fear of each other as they headed for the bush- and tree-covered ground. There the speed and heat of the flames would be less fierce.

At one point, the spreading fire had curved its path like horns to the left and right and almost joined in front. In the center, Silwana, the lion, had missed his wife and cubs. He turned to see if they were safe, but he hesitated just too long. The two horns of the fiery path met in front of him.

The lion was trapped, and well he knew it. There was, however, a narrow space to the side where the grass grew shorter and more sparsely on the hard-baked clay. Silwana had decided to risk a breakthrough there when he heard a squeak from an anthill nearby.

It was Vundhla, the hare, who greeted him. "Take it easy there, Uncle, take it easy. You will never get through that way. Come to the shelter of this grassy anthill. No fire can touch us here. Did not the witch doctor, Mpisi, give me his best fire medicine only yesterday?"

Everybody had heard of Mpisi, the hyena, and all had great faith in his medicines. He could move without a sound and could not be seen, except when the sun was very bright. Surely, he was a great witch doctor. All the veld people—the animals of the open country—went to him for his charms.

This was luck, indeed, and Silwana was glad to accept Vundhla's kind offer while the fire approached from all directions. The lion sat down with a sigh of relief. But he sprang to his four feet again as he glanced aside to see Vundhla disappearing down an aardvark hole. Silwana heard a burst of foolish laughter coming up from deep down in the earth below him.

"So that was Vundhla's game to trap me!" he roared. With a mighty leap through the licking flames, the lion managed to reach the burned area on the other side.

But what a wretched-looking lion! The flames had caught his big bushy mane, which had been his great pride. Eyebrows and whiskers were burned off; the beautiful black tuft of hair at the end of his tail was completely gone. All this lost just because he had allowed himself to be tricked by Vundhla the Clown.

It would be months before this lion could once more walk with pride among the other animals. He made a vow to get even with Mr. Vundhla.

Well, two months had passed, and Silwana's coat looked a great deal better, though it had not reached its full length and warmth.

When one day Silwana was caught in a heavy shower of rain, he still felt rather naked and cold. He bounded with haste to a stony little hill nearby, where he knew of a small snug cave. In there he would be out of the rain and could have a nice quiet sleep until the storm was over.

Having reached the cave, the lion stood in the entrance, shaking the water from his ears and looking around.

Could his eyes be deceiving him? There in a corner, trying to make himself invisible like Mpisi, the hyena, stood Vundhla. His long ears drooped with fear, and in spite of the warmth of the cave, he shivered. Well did the hare know that he had no reason to expect mercy from Silwana.

The lion licked his lips and said, "Well, Vundhla, I have got you where I want you at last! And I have waited quite a long time to get even with you. You made all the animals laugh at me these last two months. Now in a very short while they will know what has happened to you. And you will be the one they laugh at then! You are too small to make a breakfast for me, but you should taste good."

Silwana flicked his tail first to one side and then to the other. As he spoke, the noise of the rain stopped suddenly. He turned his head to see the sun burst out from beneath a cloud.

As the lion turned, Vundhla—quick as the eye can travel—jumped across the cave to a place where the roof was low. There he pretended to hold up the rock above his head, shouting, "Uncle, Uncle, the cave is falling in! Please come and help me hold the roof up. Come quickly or we will both be crushed."

Silwana covered the distance in one bound and

placed his big paws against the rocky roof. Together the pair pushed upward with all their strength, until after a time the hare said, "Uncle, my arms are thinner than yours and not so strong. They are very sore and tired. Let me collect some rocks to build a pillar to the roof to ease your arms and mine. Then we can both sit down and rest. Please hold the roof up while I get the rocks." And he vanished through the mouth of the cave.

When a long time had passed, and Vundhla had not returned with the stones, Silwana began to think he had been tricked once more.

Silwana thereupon stopped pushing against the roof and jumped backward. He landed well beyond the opening of the cave.

Nothing happened, and the roof still stayed up. Now Silwana knew he had been tricked again.

The sun shone brightly after the storm, and soon the lion again heard laughter. "Uncle," the hare shouted, "what are you having for breakfast today?"

Published as "The Hare Outwits the Lion" in *Matabele Fireside Tales,* London, Bailey Bros. & Swinfen, 1962. In his foreword, R. C. Tredgold notes the similarity between some of these tales and those known as Uncle Remus stories in the United States.

Why the Hippopotamus
Left the Forest

In the forest lands of Rhodesia, in the long years gone by, there lived a large and hairy creature, Mvuu the hippopotamus.

In those days the hippopotamus lived as the other creatures lived, in the forest lands. Mvuu was the owner of a very fine coat of nut-brown hair, of which he was extremely proud.

With bushy tail waving grandly, regularly at noontime Mvuu would take his daily stroll to the river for his midday drink. He nodded and chatted to all the creatures whom he met on the way. And day after day he would ask them if they did not consider that his was the most beautiful coat and tail in the forest.

The monkeys in the treetops were foolish enough to agree with anything if they heard it often enough. They would answer the hippo in chorus, "Well said, O noble friend. Great is your beauty. Strong are your limbs, and beautiful is your silky brown hair. Justified is your pride. O exquisite, beautiful one!"

The monkeys would throw garlands of vines from the treetops, and these Mvuu would wear around his foolish neck, taking in their flattery and praise.

Day by day his pride increased. Finally it became clear to the forest dwellers that Mvuu would become completely insufferable if he were not taken down a peg or two.

After a long and deep drink, Mvuu would sit at the side of his favorite pool and gaze with joy at the reflection in the water of his beautiful hairy coat.

Now, this was nobody's business but his own. But Mvuu brought about his downfall by not keeping his very large mouth shut.

"Ha-ha-ha," he would laugh as he sat there. "The monkeys are right. I certainly have decent-sized ears, a decent-sized tail, legs of a decent length, and a beautiful figure. Not like that foolish hare, Vundhla, who has a ridiculously small tail, foolishly long ears, completely unbalanced legs, and what a starved little body!"

Unfortunately for the hippo, the hare's long ears often caught the sound of Mvuu's hearty laughter and mocking remarks about him. These remarks annoyed the hare more and more, until one day he could stand it no longer. Vundhla decided to teach this rude fellow a lesson.

With very great cunning, the hare started to make his plans. First he laid in a store of tinder-dry grass. This he carried and stacked in a big circle around the patch of forest in which the hippo had made his sleeping quarters.

"What are you doing that for?" the hippo asked suspiciously when he saw the hare putting a large armful of grass in place one evening.

"Well, winter is nearly upon us," answered the hare, "and I thought that a wall of this grass around your sleeping quarters would keep the cold wind from ruffling your beautiful coat."

"Very thoughtful of you," agreed the hippo. "Of course a coat and tail as beautiful as mine should, in the interests of everybody, be protected against all bad weather. I am glad to know that you realize your responsibilities. Good night." And the hippo settled down with a yawn.

Now the hare went away still angry, but looking very smug and determined. "Just you wait, my friend," he muttered to himself.

His first stop was at a small village in a little clearing up a hill nearby. Here he hid himself among the brushwood that formed part of the goat kraal. Soon he saw the people gather around the evening pot of food, while the village dogs waited expectantly for the porridge scrapings.

"This is my chance," said the hare. With a hop, skip and a jump, he made for the doorway of the nearest hut. Yes, he was lucky. Just what he wanted.

There was a smouldering fire in the middle of the hut. And, joy of joys, a broken clay pot was lying nearby. He carefully selected two bits of broken pot and clapped a glowing piece of wood between them. With these tucked safely under his arm, he made all speed for the forest.

With great care, so as not to put out the precious embers he was carrying, he crept to the hippo's resting place. With equal care, he set fire at many points to the circle of dry grass that he had so carefully laid. There was a soft breeze blowing, and soon a loud crackling began.

With a grunt and a roar the hippo woke up and dashed wildly from side to side, only to be met at each turn by the tall, licking flames.

At last Mvuu was pressed to the very center of his resting place, and there the flames caught his beautiful nut-brown coat. Like a ball of flames, he rushed through the now-blazing forest. Into his favorite pool the hippo plunged, just in time to save his life.

With terror in his heart, Mvuu stayed under the water for as long as his breath lasted.

When his lungs were close to bursting for air, Mvuu rose to the surface, putting only his eyes and nose above the water. But he ducked down again in haste as the hot breath from the fire seared his burned nose and face.

In time, when the fire had died down, and the hissing and the crackling had ceased, Mvuu ventured to crawl out onto the bank.

He was very stiff and sore; but he was alive. He could almost afford to laugh at the hare for his clumsy trickery.

But could he? What was that?

Mvuu caught sight of himself in the mirror of the pool from which he had just risen. Could he believe his eyes? What were those silly little blobs where his silky ears had been? All the hair gone, and the edges frizzled away! No wonder they had been so painful.

He turned to look at his lovely tail. Not a hair left on it either, or on his bare gray body!

In shame, Mvuu quickly returned to the pool once more. As he sank out of sight, Mvuu breathed all the air out of his body so that he would sink more easily. The noise this made was as though he had said "Mvuu." And forever after, that has been the hippo's name.

And thus Mvuu has spent his days, leaving only his eyes and his nose above the water, lest the animals that had known him in his glory, should laugh at him in his shame.

From that day to this, Mvuu has been a creature of the rivers and lakes, coming out of the water only at nighttime to walk and to graze on the fringes of the forest.

This story from *Matabele Fireside Tales* was originally titled "Which Tells of How the Hippopotamus Left the Forest Lands and Became a Creature of the Rivers and Lakes."

The Hare's Rope Trick

VUNDHLA, THE HARE, HAS ALWAYS BEEN ONE FOR playing jokes. None of the creatures of the wilds trusts him, though time and again they still fall victim to his sweet words.

It happened that one day Vundhla came across the great hippopotamus, grazing peacefully on the bank of the big river.

"Good morning, Uncle," said Vundhla in his kindest tones. "You look fine and powerful this morning."

Mvuu, the hippopotamus, was well aware of his own ugliness. But he prided himself on his strong legs. His pleasure was great when people remarked on his strength.

"Yes," answered Mvuu, "it is well known by all that I am the strongest of all the animals. None can pit his strength against mine."

"Yet, Uncle," boasted Vundhla, "for all my small size and the thinness of my legs, I can beat you in a tug-of-war."

"Go away—yours is silly talk," answered Mvuu. "Whoever heard of a ridiculous little thing like you beating one of the race of Mvuu in a pulling contest?"

"There is a very special medicine for strength given to me by Mpisi the witch doctor. You must know well the strength of *his* medicines."

Vundhla was in a wicked mood. The more the hippo laughed at such foolishness, the more Vundhla begged Mvuu to test his strength. In the end, Mvuu agreed for the sake of peace to the tug-of-war.

Vundhla went off dancing with joy to braid a long, strong rope from a creeping grass that grew on a bank nearby. He told Mvuu to wait until his return.

When he had made his rope, Vundhla tied it with care to one of Mvuu's legs. He carried the other end of the rope over a little hill nearby and called, "When I say *pull*, you must really pull—for I am going to beat you!"

Having carried the rope over the rise where Mvuu could not see, Vundhla crept up to the rhinoceros, Chipembere, who was sleeping. Vundhla also carried a handful of fierce little red ants, well wrapped in a leaf. These he carefully put one by one into the ear of the sleeping rhinoceros.

After a few minutes, Chipembere sat up with a jerk and began to shake his head and scratch his ear.

When Vundhla could stop his laughter, he went up to Chipembere and said in his sweetest voice, "Good day, Uncle. I was just coming to warn you that you are sleeping near the home of the little red devils. I see one now, coming out of your ear. Let me remove it for you."

With a great show of care, Vundhla instead of taking any of the insects out, pushed the remaining ants further into the rhinoceros' ear.

"That was good of you," said Chipembere, not knowing what the hare had done. "Your paw is of a size that can fit with comfort into my ear. My own big foot has difficulty with such small matters."

"Maybe my feet are small, Uncle, but I am very strong," boasted Vundhla. "Let me tie this piece of rope around your leg and I will pull you right over that little rise."

Chipembere laughed a long time at Vundhla's boasting as he moved to another grassy bed, away from the ants' nest he supposed to be there.

But Vundhla followed him, dragging his long rope after him. He begged, "Come on, Uncle, I am feeling as strong as ten oxen today. Please have a tug-of-war with me."

"Oh, all right," said the rhinoceros good-naturedly. After all, Vundhla had helped in the matter
of the ants. So he stretched out one of his hind legs
and Vundhla lost no time in tying the rope round it.

"Now," said Vundhla, "when I get to the top of
that little rise I will shout *pull*. And when I say pull,
I mean pull—or I will pull you right into the Zambezi River!"

Chipembere laughed aloud at the hare's boasting and settled down for another doze. But as the
ants worked deeper and deeper into his ear, a new
scratching began.

Meanwhile, Vundhla took himself off to the top
of the rise, hid in the grass, and shouted, "Pull!"

As the words left the hare's mouth, all the ants
began to bite at the same time. With a roar of rage,
the rhinoceros bolted, dragging Mvuu, who had been
quietly sleeping at the other end of the rope, halfway
up the rise. And then a great pulling began!

Vundhla laughed so loudly that Mvuu and
Chipembere stopped their tug-of-war and turned to
see where the noise came from.

There at the top of the rise was Vundhla, holding his sides with mirth. Each knew then that he had
been tricked!

With lowered head and rage in his heart, each beast from his own side charged up the rise. The hippopotamus and the rhinoceros hoped to trample the wicked hare to death so that no one would ever know what fools he had made of them.

Vundhla, however, was too quick for them. He jumped to the side as the big animals met head on at the top of the hill. The crash of their collision was like a loud clap of thunder.

The earth shook and the birds flew off in terror.

Now in a tremendous rage one against the other, Mvuu and Chipembere commenced a bitter fight. To this day, the wild folk still talk of it.

After a time, though, Mvuu and Chipembere caught sight of Vundhla rolling on the ground with laughter. This reminded them of the cause of their trouble. They thereupon charged at Vundhla. But you know the speed of the hare—the more they chased, the more he laughed at them and dodged them, telling all whom he saw of the foolishness of their quarrel.

And to this day, Chipembere thinks that the fierce little red ants are still in his ears. Some say they went even further and now live in his brain, and it is this that makes the rhinoceros so uncertain in his temper.

And Mvuu, the hippopotamus? He searches up and down the riverbanks, hoping that one day he will catch Vundhla and throw him to the ever-waiting crocodiles.

This story, taken from *Matabele Fireside Tales,* is one of the better-known Bantu tales and available in several versions.

The Tortoise Who Dared the Hare

FUDU, THE TORTOISE, WAS EATING JUICY BULB
leaves near Ramba fountain, which is surrounded by
tall palm trees.

The tortoise was enjoying his breakfast. He
would soon close his eyes and go to sleep for the day.
But as he decided to crawl into a clump of grass
nearby, he heard the patter, patter of light feet.
There in front of him stood Vundhla, the hare.

"Good morning, Uncle," said Vundhla. "I'm
sorry to disturb you, but I have come for a drink of
water."

"Help yourself," said Fudu, and watched while
Vundhla drank.

But Vundhla was in a mischievous mood, and he decided to have some fun with Fudu.

"Uncle," he teased, "those are funny little legs that you have. I am sure you couldn't run any distance on them. Look at my beautiful long legs. None of the animals can catch me. When they do get a bit near, I just pop down a hole. Ha, ha, ha!"

"Look here, Vundhla," replied Fudu. "My legs suit me, and I can beat you in a race. Your long thin legs could not even carry my house—much less win a race!"

Vundhla rolled on the ground and squeaked with merriment. When he stopped laughing, he suggested that they have a race there and then.

"Uncle," the hare said, "we will run as far as that tall palm tree. It is only a hundred yards away. If you beat me, I will give you my favorite ox that I value more than all my cattle."

The tortoise thought the matter over. He wanted to win the race and get even with the boastful hare. He hit upon a plan.

"When I run, Vundhla," Fudu said, "I prefer miles, not yards. I will race you to Mushenje's Pan, which is only six miles away. You know the path. We will start from the water hole when the sun reaches noon. If you win the race, you can choose the best ox in my herd. Let me see—today is Monday. We will run on Saturday. Now go away. I want to sleep."

Vundhla agreed to the arrangement. He knew where the water basin called Mushenje's Pan was. He went home laughing.

The tortoise wasted no time. As soon as Vundhla was out of sight, Fudu sent out messages to all his tortoise relatives. He told the tortoises how they could help him in his plan.

On Saturday, the tortoises were to place themselves at regular intervals along the path to the water basin. One tortoise would wait at the starting point, at Ramba fountain. The others would wait just over small rises along the path the race was to take. They were all to commence running toward the goal. They were to watch the road carefully, and when Vundhla had raced past, they could go back about their own business.

Fudu made sure each tortoise understood thoroughly the part he was to play. He then took a gourd with him and started out for Mushenje's Pan. He arrived at the water hole on Saturday and filled his gourd with water. Then he set off along the path *toward* the starting point.

Vundhla, the hare, arrived at the starting point on time on Saturday, and so did Fudu's cousin, who of course looked exactly like Fudu. The tortoise and the hare shook hands and the race began. Vundhla was so swift that he was out of sight in a few moments. Fudu's cousin lost interest—though it was a long while before he could stop laughing.

Vundhla was laughing, too, until he came to the top of the first little rise ahead. There he saw the second tortoise plodding along in front of him. Vund-

hla, of course thinking the tortoise was Fudu, put on
extra speed and was soon out of sight. But he could
not understand just how Fudu had managed to get
ahead of him.

Another little hill and another, and each time
Fudu was ahead. The tortoise always laughed loudly
as the hare passed him. By this time, Vundhla firmly
believed that the tortoise had learned to fly!

The sun was boiling now, and Mushenje's Pan
was still two miles away. Another rise, and still Fudu
was ahead! Oh, why, Vundhla thought, had he left
Ramba fountain, where the water was cool and
sweet? And his favorite ox seemed likely to be lost
as well.

The hare was drawing near the water hole, however, so he put on his last spurt of speed. His breath-
ing was heavy and his throat was dry. Crash! Vundhla tripped and fell head over heels, then lay
exhausted where he had fallen. He just could not go
any further.

The hare fell alseep, with every limb trembling
from the strain. When he awakened, he managed to
get to his feet and staggered on until he could see the
winning post with the stretch of cool water beyond.

But what was that? Someone was coming

toward him, carrying a gourd of water. And that someone was Fudu! This was more than Vundhla could face, and he fainted.

Some time later Vundhla recovered to find that he had been sprinkled with cool water. He felt a great deal better. He opened his eyes to find Fudu holding a gourd to his lips and heard him say in a soothing voice, "Take a drink of this, Son, I had an idea you would be needing it!"

Originally titled "A Race Between the Tortoise and the Hare" in *Matabele Fireside Tales,* this tale is like the famous fable only in the hare's defeat. The basic trick by which the hare is outwitted is the same the turtle used to vanquish the beaver in a Seneca Indian tale retold by Arthur C. Parker in *Skunny Wundy.*

How the Bat Made His Choice

IT HAS BEEN HANDED DOWN BY THE ANCESTORS THAT before the big drought struck, Lulwane, the bat, had his place among the bird people. He was looked up to because of the beauty of his many-colored feathers. But those who liked him were few, for his greed and his selfishness were known by all.

When food was scarce, Lulwane would never share his feeding grounds with others. He would leave the tree roosts while it was still dark, so that no one should see him go.

The big drought came. As the months wore on and still no rain fell to swell the hard dry fruit or fill the failing pools, Lulwane grew sleek and fat while most creatures starved. Finally he was driven from the other birds because of his greed. He took refuge in a cave.

Earlier and earlier, Lulwane began his secret trips to his store of food. His flights were swift, almost as quick as the eye can travel. He did not stop on the way, for he no longer wished to meet anyone like himself.

Soon Lulwane had eyesight like those who see by night. By day, he lived in caves and dark places where he could rest undisturbed and the sun would not hurt his eyes.

But although his secret food store filled Lulwane's eating needs, he could not find water. And of what good is food when there is no water? Dew there was, that fell by night. But this rolled off the leaves before Lulwane could even wet the tip of his beak.

All beasts and birds were in a sorry state.

Now, one tribe among the rest had brains beyond the other tribes. This was that of Gundwane, the rat. Besides brains, the rats also had hands. And who is afraid to work when his throat is dry?

It therefore happened that the rat people worked together to smooth out a large and gently sloping basin in the earth. They pounded it well with small clenched fists. They worked in clay from the deeper water holes where the bottoms were still damp. Thus the rats planned to catch and hold the dew that nightly escaped them.

With deft and careful hands, the great crowd of rat people built a dew pond. Some carried the clay, others carefully worked it into the dry and crumbling earth to make smooth walls.

Soon the rats' task was done, and no longer did the precious dew sink from sight. It slowly trickled down the sloping sides of the basin and gathered in a pool for all to drink.

Great was the rejoicing among both birds and beasts! At dawn each day, a long procession gathered to quench their thirsts. Loud were the praises of the clever rat tribe.

"Now," said Lulwane, "I will leave my kind forever and become like the rat. For who among the bird people could have provided water to satisfy the thirsts of all? Surely Gundwane has brains and skill beyond the rest."

Therefore Lulwane came earlier and earlier to drink. He came when it was still dark and drank when the rat people drank. Night by night, he grew more like them, both in looks and voice as he crept about among them around the water's edge.

When the sun rose, the rats returned to their holes in the ground, and there they spent the daylight hours. This Lulwane could not do, so he always flew away as the first light greeted the day and sought the refuge of caves and dark places.

Since Lulwane found no bough on which to perch within these caves, he clutched the roof. There he hung upside down, and thus he sleeps today.

In time, through long absence from the sun, Lulwane's many-colored feathers failed to grow and lost the brilliance of their color. Shorter and shorter the sun-starved feathers became, and duller and duller, until they were a dingy gray.

To protect himself from the cold found within the caves, Lulwane grew a covering of fur. His wings became webbed, and his beak grew short to form the mouth he has today. But still the bat flies with speed, and who is to deny he was once a bird?

Originally titled "Brother to the Rat" in *Matabele Fireside Tales*. It is interesting to note that the Matabele teller explained the bat was often called "close-to-the-ear" from its ability to fly close to but not touch whatever is in its path.

Tales Told in Malawi and Kenya

The Bushbuck's Visitor

ONCE UPON A TIME, A BUSHBUCK LIVED IN A NEAT little house on the bank of a river. This small antelope with spiral horns had formed a friendship with a goat, and the two animals often visited one another.

After calling upon his friend one day, the bushbuck returned to his home to find the door shut. He heard a strange and very harsh voice coming from inside the house.

"Who is in the bushbuck's house?" asked the owner of the house, the bushbuck.

"It is I, the eater of bushbucks," replied a rasping voice. "Be ready, for I am coming to eat you!"

The bushbuck was greatly alarmed. Turning, he ran as fast as his legs would carry him to tell his friend the goat about the dreadful monster in his house.

On his way, the bushbuck met an elephant, who exclaimed in surprise, "Friend, never have I seen anyone so frightened as you. Why are you in such a hurry on this fine and sunny morning?"

"There is a wicked monster in my house," panted the bushbuck. "He says that he is coming out to eat me!" And the bushbuck made ready to run on.

The elephant laughed loudly at the bushbuck's fear. "What utter nonsense," he said. "I will go and see for myself."

The elephant went boldly to the river, while the bushbuck turned to watch events.

"Who is in the bushbuck's house?" the elephant called out from a distance.

He was greeted by a deep voice which croaked, "It is I, the eater of elephants. Be ready, for I am coming out to eat you!"

The elephant thought that, judging by the sound of the voice, this was surely an even larger monster than himself. So, after a terrified look all around him, he tore off into the forest with his trunk

in the air, knocking down trees both left and right in his haste. The bushbuck ran along ahead of him.

The animals had not gone far before they met a lion. "Well, well, well, my friend!" said the lion in surprise to the elephant. "Whoever has been bold enough to put such a big creature as you to flight?"

"There is a terrible monster in the bushbuck's house," stammered the elephant breathlessly. "I— I laughed at the bushbuck when he told me about this, good Simba, but I find that he spoke the truth and his fears are fully justified. It is a dreadful monster, good Simba."

"Come," said the lion good-naturedly. "The three of us will go together to see who dares to frighten such a respected and enormous member of the forest as you."

After a great deal of persuasion, the two trembling animals agreed to return with the lion to investigate the matter. Thereupon, all three made their way to the little house by the river.

"Who is in the bushbuck's house?" roared the lion in a thunderous voice.

"It is I, the eater of lions!" came the harsh, grating reply. "Be ready, for I am coming out to eat you!"

"What! To eat the king of the forest?" bellowed

the lion. "Then come and eat me, for I am not afraid of you!"

There was muffled laughter from inside the hut. The lion pushed aside the door to see a fat old frog sitting in the middle of the floor, chuckling and croaking to himself.

"So!" said the lion, greatly amused, "You are the dangerous monster who has dared to frighten my two friends?"

And the lion called together all the animals from the forest and told them of the cowardice of the bushbuck and the elephant. These two became the laughingstock of the country.

From that day onward, the elephant has been ashamed of himself and has looked upon the lion as his superior. And this is in spite of the fact that he, the elephant, is the largest creature in the wilds.

This story from an Agikuyu tribal source was collected in Kenya. It is called "The Bushbuck's House" in *Fireside Tales from the North,* published by Howard Timmins in Cape Town, 1966.

The Lion and
the Little Brown Bird

TWO COMPLETELY DIFFERENT CREATURES OF THE
wilds sometimes formed a friendship. Once there was
such a friendship between Ngango, the tawny-
maned lion, and Timba, the common little brown
robin of Nyasaland.

It began when Timba noticed that from time to
time the lion made kills that were too large for him
to finish at one meal. This meant that part of the
meat was left to spoil—and such meat meant big,
juicy white maggots. These worms were Timba's favorite food.

It was therefore not surprising that Timba began to follow Ngango from one hunting ground to

another. The little bird listened intently for the lion's cry of victory each time he made a kill.

"This is my hunting ground, this is my hunting ground!" the lord of the forest would roar. He stood majestically on the top of the highest ant heap that he could find to let all the creatures far and wide know that they were to bow to him in homage. Of course, no one dreamed of contradicting him, least of all the little brown robin.

The lion, on his part, had no objection to Timba benefiting from what he left. Day after day, the big cat would chat in a friendly way with the little brown bird who sat in the tree above, twittering in excited anticipation.

"Tii-tii-tii, tii-tii-tii," trilled the bird, his song filling the countryside with music. "Great is the strength of Ngango! Wise is the rule of his law!" Then one day he added sadly, "But oh, why am I so small and unimportant?"

Ngango was in a particularly good mood that morning. He was pleased to listen to Timba's flattering song, so he interrupted it.

"Yes, my friend, all that you sing of me is true, and it is indeed unfortunate that you are of so little account. If you were of greater importance, your song would mean more to my subjects. But why do you stoop to eating my spoiled leavings instead of hunting good red meat of your own?"

"Indeed, good Ngango, I agree with all that you say," answered the little bird unhappily. "But I am too small to catch anything else. Oh, that I were bigger and stronger and fiercer!"

"I can help you to become so, should you wish," said the lion pleasantly.

"O Lord of the Forest, Mighty One, please do so," trilled the little bird in an excited voice.

"Then we must visit Fisi, the witch doctor," said the lion. "Come, I will take you to him."

They found Fisi, the hyena, lying asleep at the entrance to his bone-littered cave. The lion's loud greeting sent the ugly creature scuttling into the shadows.

"Fisi, my brave fellow!" laughed the lion as the hyena nervously shuffled back to the cave entrance to discover what had frightened him.

"I have some work for you to do," the lion continued. "Our friend Timba is tired of being so small and insignificant that he is forced to eat the worms in the leavings of other people's kills. He wishes to be changed into a fierce animal that can catch and kill meat for himself. Please mix a suitable potion for him."

The hyena went back into the gloom of his untidy cave and soon returned with the desired mixture, which he gave to the robin.

No sooner had the bird swallowed it than he changed into Lilongwe, the fierce little gray mongoose. He was delighted and immediately went into the forest to hunt rats, birds, and other small creatures.

Things went well to begin with, and Lilongwe was satisfied. But after a while the lion and the mongoose met.

"Well, Lilongwe, how are you getting on?" asked the lion.

"Not so well as I could wish," grumbled the mongoose. "Birds are difficult to catch. Besides, it is animal flesh that I crave. If only Fisi had mixed a stronger potion for me."

"Very well," said the lion with an indulgent smile. "We will visit Fisi again to see if he will help you further."

The animals repeated their visit to the witch doctor's cave. Fisi mixed another magic brew at the lion's request.

No sooner had the mongoose swallowed the potion than in his place stood a sleek and velvety spotted leopard. Nyalugwe, now his name, purred with pride and pleasure and at once bounded into the forest to hunt small buck, hares, and baboons.

For some time the leopard was contented with his lot. But eventually he thought how very much more exciting it would be to hunt in the open by daylight instead of keeping to shadows of the dark forest, as was the habit of the leopards. Besides, he wanted to kill big animals such as eland and buffalo, not stupid little things like baboons and rock rabbits. The more he thought about the matter, the more dissatisfied he became.

It was not long after this that Ngango saw Nyalugwe slinking along a forest path one morning just after sunrise.

"Good morning, my friend," the lion greeted him. "Now are you satisfied?"

"Not completely," replied the leopard ungraciously. "I wish I could catch big animals, as you do."

"Very well," said the lion patiently, "we will visit Fisi once more." And the two went to the witch doctor's cave for the third time.

When the hyena had prepared an extra large potion, the lion took it. Before handing it to Nyalugwe, he said, "I must make one condition before your next change takes place. When you have made your kills, you are never, *never ever* to roar as I do because, as you are well aware, all the hunting in

this area belongs to me. In my roar I am entitled to
say, 'This is my hunting ground, this is my hunting
ground!' and no one has the right to challenge me.
You must say, 'This is Ngango's hunting ground, this
is Ngango's hunting ground!' If you disobey this
order, you will be punished. Do you understand?"

The leopard sulkily thumped the ground on
each side of him with his long elegant tail, banded
with yellow and black. After he had promised to follow the lion's instruction, Ngango handed him the
magic potion.

The leopard could hardly wait to gulp the mixture down. Immediately there stood in his stead a
fine young lion, strong and well built, but smaller
than his friend.

Soundlessly the young lion slipped into the tall
grass at the edge of the forest and began at once to
stalk and hunt big game upon the plains.

His first kill was an antelope, the following day
he killed a young kudu cow. This was life indeed!
How proud he felt as he dragged the various kills to
the top of an anthill, as he had seen Ngango do.

He announced for all to hear, "This is Ngango's
hunting ground, this is Ngango's hunting ground!"
before settling down to his meal.

The big lion heard him and was pleased to be treated with the respect he deserved. "The young lion will surely be satisfied with his lot now," the older lion thought to himself.

The young lion went from one success to another, and the animals he killed became larger and larger. Finally he pulled down a big buffalo bull.

"Surely," he said to himself with pride as he dragged the bull to the highest point that he could find, "I am now a match for any creature living. I have as much right to this hunting ground as any other lion." And he roared for all to hear, "This is *my* hunting ground, this is *my* hunting ground!"

The king of the wilds heard this boastful roar and hastened to where the young lion was tearing chunks of meat from his kill.

"What did I hear you roar?" the older lion asked in a chilling tone as he bared his great yellow teeth.

Ngango looked so angry that the young lion's heart missed a beat or two. Perhaps after all, he thought, it had been rather unwise of him to declare his strength quite so soon. Maybe he should have waited until he had reached his full power and was certain that he could overcome the mighty Ngango.

"I spoke without thinking," he said hesitantly.

"That is no excuse!" growled Ngango. "Tell me," he continued in a pleasanter tone, "what were you before Fisi changed you into a lion?"

"I was a leopard," mumbled the ungrateful animal.

What happened next happened so quickly that the young lion was not aware of the change until it had taken place. Looking down at his paws, he saw the spotted fur of the leopard, to which he had returned.

His head reeled, but he was brought back to his senses when the old lion asked, "And before you were a leopard, what were you?"

"I was a mongoose," muttered the leopard, now anything but sure of himself. He was startled to see how enormous Ngango had suddenly become—until he realized that it was he who had grown small. He was once more Lilongwe, the fierce little gray mongoose.

But the lion had not finished with him yet. "Yes, of course you were. I was forgetting," the lord of the wilds said. "And before that?"

"I was a little bird," faltered the mongoose.

Hardly had the words left his mouth before he was again Timba, the tiny little insignificant brown bird who long ago had sung for the powerful beast staring at him.

"Tii-tii-tii," he chirped as he fluttered up into the tree above the lion to begin once more his search for juicy white worms.

This Ngoni story from Malawi is called "The Lion and the Robin" and credit is given by Phyllis Savory to James Banda as narrator in *Fireside Tales from the North*. The importance of the witch doctor's magic is typical of these tales. The ending recalls the downfall of another too-ambitious character in the European folktale of "The Fisherman's Wife."

How a Poor Man Was Rewarded

LONG, LONG AGO, THERE LIVED A POOR MAN AND his wife. Because they had no possessions of their own, the husband had to search the forests for the food they ate. Sometimes it would mean a meal of roots and berries, but occasionally he was fortunate enough to catch a bird or animal in one of the many traps and snares he set along the animal trails.

There was, however, a large and very beautiful bird which, although the man saw it every day, proved too clever to be caught in even his most carefully hidden trap.

This bird seemed to mock the man as it remained just out of range of his bow and arrow. Eventually the husband determined that come what may, he would capture this bird.

One day the man was just about to return home empty-handed and even hungrier than usual when he remembered a trap he had failed to visit. He retraced his steps and upon reaching the trap, he gave a shout of joy. There, securely caught by a leg, was the lovely bird that had fooled him so often.

The husband rushed forward. Seizing the bird by the neck to choke back its cries, he said, "Today I have got you, my friend!" Thereupon he took out his knife and prepared to kill the bird, thankful he would have at least something, if only a bird, to take back to his wife that evening.

"Mercy, human, mercy!" gasped the poor creature as the man's grip on its throat tightened. "Spare my life, and you have my word that you will not regret your kindness."

The man loosened his grasp and stepped back in surprise the better to view the rare and golden plumaged bird that spoke to him.

The bird continued, "Although my only earthly possessions are these golden feathers that cover me, yet in them lies a magic. It will provide you with both food and drink forevermore. Release me, good human, for the thong of the trap that holds me has cut painfully."

Now this was a difficult situation in which the man found himself. What if the bird was lying to him? Why, he would lose the precious food the bird would provide to keep the man and his wife from hunger for at least a day or two.

Yet the bird itself might have a mate and maybe even young ones. They would wait anxiously for the bird's return, hungry too and hoping for food.

But suppose the bird spoke the truth? Why, the man would be able to sit back in idleness forever-more. There would be riches beyond counting.

Besides, who had ever heard of a bird able to speak as man to man?

The husband decided that he would take the risk. He untied the thong that had cut so deeply into the poor bird's leg.

Thankfully, the lovely bird stretched its aching legs. Then carefully the bird pulled a golden-colored feather from each wing and gave them to its deliverer.

"With this gift, human," the bird said, "I also give you words of warning. If you wish to keep the magic of these feathers, you must neither speak nor boast to others of your good fortune. Should you do so, the power of my gift will vanish and you will be left as poor as you are today. Do not treat my warning lightly. Wish as you hold these feathers in your hands, and they will fulfill your every desire."

The man thanked the bird for its gift and hastened home. As he hurried along the path, he wished that he would find food in plenty waiting for him at his journey's end. Which would he find, the man wondered, starvation or plenty?

The golden bird was as good as its word. Inside the man's hut his food vessels were full to overflowing. The dried-up spring nearby gushed forth its water once more, and his wife was spared her daily walk of many miles to the only water hole they knew.

Life smiled upon the couple at last, and the husband was able to idle the days away, wishing for all the things that made life sweet, and they came to him in plenty.

Many times the woman questioned her husband as to how it came about that although their neglected garden was not yet tilled and ready for the hoped-for rains, he no longer hunted in the forest. And yet she always found food in her cooking pots and luxuries as well.

But each time his wife questioned him, the man avoided an explanation.

At last, as so often happens when life becomes too easy, the man grew careless in what he said. He boasted to all around of his wealth.

The woman grew increasingly suspicious of their good fortune. "Husband," she finally nagged him, "you show no astonishment at our wealth. You must be hiding something from me. Maybe at night-time while I sleep you steal the good things that I find cooking upon our fire. Surely you must have secret dealings with the evil one to bring sparkling water bubbling from the parched earth when all else is dry. I must ask our tribal witch doctor to satisfy me about these two matters."

Now the mention of a witch doctor—or smeller-out—struck terror into the heart of her simple hus-band. He had no wish for dealings with things he did not understand.

"Wife," he begged, "do not call the witch doctor. By his arts he will surely find the magic feathers that provide us with all the good things we have. You will then lose me as well, for enemies will certainly kill me to obtain the magic of my golden feathers for themselves."

Too late the man remembered the parting warn-ing of the bird. He realized that not only had he shared his secret with his wife but that he had boasted to others of his riches.

It was with deep dread on the next day that he held the feathers and wished his daily wishes.

His worst fears were confirmed when all his wishes remained unfulfilled. Hastening to his bubbling spring, he found only drying mud. Once more, the couple felt the pangs of hunger, and once again the husband was obliged to set his traps along the paths in the forest.

Life was harder even than before because the prolonged dry period made food even more difficult to find.

One day while the poor man was visiting his traps as usual he met his neighbor with his dog.

"We will hunt together," said the man, pleased to have company as he continued his rounds.

To the man's great surprise, they found the same golden bird caught in a snare.

The poor man rushed toward it, exclaiming, "Once more you are in my power, O golden bird, for I have caught you again! Give me two more of your magic feathers and I will release you."

"Spare my life a second time, good human," begged the bird.

At once the man untied the noose of the snare that held the golden bird. But no sooner had he loosened the poor creature than the neighbor's dog pounced upon it.

With difficulty, the man dragged the animal away and picked up the bird. Running to the edge of the forest, he released it without waiting for his payment of the precious golden feathers.

"Once more, human, I thank you," the bird said gratefully. "Except for your timely help, the dog would have killed me. In the past, I made you a gift of my magic feathers because you spared my life when you and your wife were hungry. But there was a condition set. That you broke that condition is no concern of mine. You have suffered for not listening to my warning, and maybe you have learned your lesson."

The bird then continued, "This time I will give all that is in my power to give, and I make no condition with my gift. The magic in these feathers will last forever, for you have not only spared my life again, you have saved it. Also you have twice trusted my word."

Plucking two more feathers, one from each wing, the bird gave them to the man, then spread its golden wings, rose up into the heavens, and was gone.

It was a happy man who returned to his wife that day. He was happy at the good fortune that had come to him again and grateful to the golden bird for rewarding his kindness to one in distress. The man was humble, too, because he had learned that his failure to heed the magic bird's warning had brought about his earlier downfall.

This Ngoni story from Malawi is called "The Man and the Bird" and credit is given by Phyllis Savory to Eline Ngoma as narrator in *Fireside Tales from the North*.

The Lazy Son

As an old Kikuyu man lay dying, he sent for his only son, Kimwaki.

"My son," the old man said, "I have lived my life, and the time has come for me to join my ancestors. My years have not been spent in idleness, for my fields are the fairest in the land. My cows have multiplied and my goats are many. All these things now belong to you. Carry me beneath the stars, for I wish to die."

Not long after this conversation, the old man died. After the burial ceremonies had taken place, Kimwaki looked around him and counted his wealth. It was, he found, great indeed for a young man.

No need to toil now, for there would be no one to prod him on. Life was very good, and the young man settled down to enjoy it in an idle, worthless way.

Day after day Kimwaki lay dreaming in the sunshine. When the sun became too hot for comfort, he lay in the shade of a big tree that grew beside his hut. He let his lovely garden become overgrown by weeds and grass. His sleek and glossy cattle, with no one to drive them to their pastures, became hollow-eyed and thin. The little goats bleated in distress, not knowing where to go.

But Kimwaki did not care, because his wise and thrifty father had left him overflowing food bins. He felt he could afford to sit back and rest. Hunger would never touch *him*. What else mattered?

In a land where it is the rule for each neighbor to help the other, not a soul lifted a finger to assist this lazy youth who gave no help to others. Thus things went from bad to worse. No one cared, and Kimwaki was shunned by all around him.

Kimwaki led this useless life for many months, until he began to tire of the loneliness.

Then one day in early spring, Kimwaki napped as usual beneath his tree. Excited twittering and singing broke into his dreams. Annoyed, he opened his eyes to see what had disturbed his pleasant slumber. Up in the tree was a flock of little weaver birds, darting here and there. They were all as busy as could be, for it was nesting time.

Spring was in the air, and the male weaver birds were building nests in which to raise their young ones. Their excited twittering and busy activity made Kimwaki open his eyes a little wider to watch the birds work together. Before long, the lazy boy came to realize the joy the birds found in cooperation.

Chattering and singing, each male bird did his share to build the colony. One would bring a tiny piece of grass, another a little twig, while yet another added a feather to his nest. Busily the birds worked, as though their very lives depended upon their speed (which of course was true). When evening came, the frames of the little nests were completed.

On the following day the same activities took place. The clever birds used their tiny beaks to weave the grasses in and out, lining the nests with the softest down.

Kimwaki watched it all as he lay beneath the big tree. By the time the second evening came, thunder-clouds were gathering in the sky. Kimwaki thought how wise the little weaver birds were to provide shelter for their babies against the coming rains.

Every day Kimwaki watched the diligent feathered workers. In a short while, a whole colony of finished nests hung from the branches of the tree. And during all this period, the lesson of the birds' cooperation and their hard work had been sinking deeper and deeper into the young man's mind.

Finally Kimwaki said to himself, "I am a big, strong young man, while they are only tiny birds. I have two big hands with which to work, while each of them has only a little beak. They are safe and sheltered, and I am not. Surely *they* are wise, and *I* am not!"

He thought the matter over during the night that followed, and next morning he rose early. Taking his rusty hoe with him, he went to the field that belonged to his nearest neighbor. There Kimwaki began to dig and clear the weeds and grass away. When this was done, he started to hoe the ground.

All day long Kimwaki worked in a friendly way with others who joined him. When evening came, he found himself singing as he returned to his dilapidated hut. He felt as happy and lighthearted as the little weaver birds!

Day after day Kimwaki went unbidden, first to the garden of one neighbor and then to another, helping where he could and asking nothing in return.

Then one morning he awoke to hear cheerful chattering and laughter coming from his own untidy, overgrown shamba, or garden. He looked out and saw that all his neighbors were as busy as could be, clearing and hoeing his weed-covered fields. He joined them at once, and soon the plot was ready for planting.

Later on, when the rains came, the same neighbors helped him plant his crops and rethatch his leaking hut.

The season progressed, and Kimwaki's crops grew. As the maize, beans, and potatoes grew, so grew his pride in achievement. The young man no longer wasted his days beneath the big tree, but continued to help those around him. He also saw to the comfort of his neglected flocks. Joyfully he watched the glow of health creep back to the dull coats of his cows and goats.

Before long, Kimwaki's crops were ready to be harvested. His willing neighbors helped him in the fields, thereby returning the help that Kimwaki had so willingly given them. And when all the grain had been winnowed and stored away, and his potatoes and beans sold, Kimwaki found to his joy that once more his father's fields had yielded the highest return in the land.

Kimwaki therefore gave thanks to the little weaver birds for showing him that only through unselfishness and hard work can peace, security, and happiness be found.

This Agikuyu story from Kenya is titled "Kimwaki and the Weaver Birds" in *Fireside Tales from the North*.

The Bird with the Golden Legs

ONCE UPON A TIME, A MAN WALKED IN HIS ORCHARDS with his two sons. He was a man of great standing among his neighbors—a chief, in fact—and he was very rich indeed. The trees in his orchards were many. However, as fast as the fruit ripened, the birds flew down from the skies and ate it all.

As the father and his sons reached the choicest tree of all, a flock of birds fluttered from it. Big birds, small birds, long birds, and short birds—many sorts and kinds rose up together into the sky.

But one bird remained behind after the rest had gone. It cocked its head first on one side, and then on the other, as it gazed intently at the father and his sons.

It was not a long bird, and it was not a short bird. But there was something about it that made it different from any bird the chief had ever seen—it had two golden legs.

And when this creature finally flew away, its speed was like lightning streaking across the sky.

The chief gazed at the bird in astonishment. "Son," he said, turning to the elder boy, "I will give you half my kingdom if you will catch that bird for me. Never have I longed so greatly to possess any living creature."

But neither upon that day, nor upon the next, did the elder boy make any effort to carry out his father's wish.

"Son," said the chief to the boy a few days later, "have you no feelings of duty toward your father? Is that why you do not try to fulfill my desire?"

"Not so, my father," replied the boy sullenly. "But do you not realize that no living soul could catch such a bird? Surely it is the brother to lightning."

"If you do not try," insisted the chief, "how can you tell me this? If you make no effort to carry out

my wish, I will disinherit you before I die and you
will be left without possessions. But if you bring the
bird to me unharmed, great wealth and happiness
shall be yours. You shall have a kingdom of your
own, with many subjects to hoe your crops and tend
your flocks. All this and more I will give to you in
return for the bird."

"Very well," answered the elder son ungraciously. "I will see what I can do."

The young man gathered all the beggars and
evildoers from the surrounding villages, and together
they departed in the direction taken by the bird. On
the following day, however, the son returned alone
and empty-handed. He told his father that he needed
money for the journey he had planned.

At first the chief refused, not trusting his first-
born's honesty.

"Then, Father," begged the younger son, "allow
me to catch the bird for you."

The chief smiled affectionately at the small boy.
He replied, "Child, you are both too young and too
small. You would die upon a journey that such a
quest would take you."

Then the elder son again approached his father.
"Father," he repeated persuasively, "give me money.

If I am to catch this bird, I will need money for our journey. We plan to follow the bird to its resting place, and this might take many months."

The youth appeared to be in earnest. So at last the old man, feeling that surely his son must love him to plan such a journey upon his behalf, gave him all he asked. And so the son and his party set out upon the search.

Day after day upon day after day, the men traveled, following the direction taken by the bird with the golden legs. For a year and a day they tramped.

Finally, weary and footsore, they came to a green and rich land. It was so beautiful and fresh, after the barren country through which they had passed that they had no wish to continue their search for the strange bird.

The oldest follower said to the chief's son, who was the youngest of them all, "Boy, we are tired. We have walked for many months upon your behalf, and yet we are no nearer to finding what we seek. Our human legs are no match against a bird's wings. We are wasting our time. Let us build a village in this pleasant land and live the lives we wish, with no one to rule us. The money that your father gave you for the search will assure us of wealth and comfort forevermore."

And so there they stayed.

When many months passed, and no news had come of the fortunes of the elder son, the younger son approached the old chief. He said, "Father, my brother has not returned, nor have we had word of him. Some evil may have befallen him and his followers. Let me go in search of him."

But his father would not let the young boy go.

Time and again the child begged to be allowed to look for his brother. Each time the chief patted the small boy's head and said, "You are still too small, my son, to leave the safety of your mother's hut."

However, eventually the younger son, now grown to a young man, persuaded his father to let him go. He left home rejoicing.

The journey was hazardous, and many adventures befell him in the two years he followed his brother's footsteps. Finally, he reached the village his brother and his men had founded.

To the boy's surprise and sorrow, he found that he was unwelcome.

"For what crafty reason have you followed us all this long way from our home?" the elder brother asked him roughly, without a word of greeting. "Unless, perhaps, you came to take back bad reports of our doings to our father? Leave this place at once or it will be the worse for you."

"The Great One guided me in your footsteps," the youth replied with spirit. "You took our father's wealth and his men, and now you plan to kill his son."

"Drive him out! Drive him out!" cried the men roughly. "There is neither food nor water in the barren land beyond. Let him die of starvation there. Then none can say we killed him."

So again the youth traveled on and on. But now he traveled with an even greater determination, for he had taken it upon himself to search for the bird with the golden legs.

Sixteen times the full moon came and passed again, and still he struggled on.

The country he traveled through was unfriendly and wild, and in sixteen months he passed only three villages. At each village the people made him welcome and begged him to stay with them forever— for in these lonely regions visitors were rare. However, each time the young man refused their hospitality. After resting for a while, he hurried on.

It was still the second son's goal to find the bird with the golden legs. He was determined to succeed.

Finally came a day when, almost dropping from exhaustion, the young traveler approached the largest and most beautiful tree he had ever seen. So green and rich was this tree and everything surrounding it that he decided to rest in the inviting shade of its spreading branches. He lay down under the tree, and pillowing his head upon his arms, he was soon fast asleep.

When he awoke, the sun was a great ball of crimson, climbing up from the horizon. The young man realized that it was almost noon. He also realized that it had been a long, long while since he had eaten. He took his bow and arrow and looked around for something to eat. But nothing came his way, and by midafternoon he was hungrier than ever.

He returned to the tree. When he looked up into its cool branches, he saw a flock of tiny birds busily eating the fruit it bore.

"Surely," the young man thought to himself, "if the birds can eat the fruit, then so can I."

He climbed up into the branches and prepared to satisfy his hunger.

But no sooner had he put the first wet berry into his mouth than a party of ugly dwarfs, led by their king, appeared beneath him. Climbing up after him, they surrounded and caught the boy. As they dragged him down, they said angrily, "Human, from where do you come and where do you go?"

"I come from afar, and I travel afar," replied the boy politely. "Please do not kill me, for it is help I need, not harm."

"Be that as it may," answered the tiny king, "you are not of our kind. You are flesh and blood, which we are not. Why should we help you?"

"I may not be of your kind, but you would not have me starve, would you?" said the boy persuasively. "I have had neither food nor drink for many days."

Perhaps it was the boy's youth that touched the heart of the little king. Upon the king's orders, his subjects carried the boy to their home. There they cared for him and fed him, while the young man told them the tale of his quest for the bird with the golden legs.

"Good fortune has guided you to this land," said the king of the dwarfs, after he had heard all that had befallen the boy since he left his father's home.

"Come," the king continued, "I will show you where to find the chief who owns the bird you seek. But the man's wealth is beyond counting, so he will not part with his magic bird unless you can offer him something better in exchange."

The boy wondered what to do, but the king added, "However, I will help you, because I see that you are wise beyond your years and possess a steadfast heart. But you must hide yourself until the moon is full, for at that time only, will it be possible for you to catch the bird by a trick, without the chief knowing."

The little king led the boy to the outskirts of the chief's village, and there he left him.

The young adventurer hid himself in the bushes and prepared for a long wait until the moon was full. But in spite of his great care, he was caught by the village headman and taken into the great chief's presence.

When at first the lad refused to answer the chief's questions, the chief asked, "What can it be that the stranger searches for, except my magic bird with the golden legs?"

Finally the boy admitted that he was searching for the bird.

"Very well," bargained the chief, "I will come to terms with you. Find me the magic knife that is as long as my arm, shines like the sun, and is forever sharp, and I will give you the bird with the golden legs."

The boy now prepared to set forth upon this further quest, for his heart was fixed upon his goal.

Before leaving, he decided to return to the home of the little dwarfs and tell them what had happened to him. It was fortunate that he did so, for the knife was in the keeping of the little king. At once he led the young man to the great tree in which they had found him.

Taking the precious knife from its hiding place among the roots, the king of the dwarfs gave it to the boy. Now he realized why the dwarfs had been so disturbed when they found him near the spot where the knife was hidden.

With a light heart, the boy now trustingly took the magic knife to the great chief. But once the knife was safely in the chief's hands, he sent the boy away —without giving him the bird.

"Now find me the bow," the chief had commanded, "and the arrow that always finds its target. Then, and only then, will I part with my magic bird."

Returning sadly to the dwarfs, the boy told them of the chief's betrayal.

The king of the dwarfs spoke with anger in his heart. "Go back along the road that leads to the chief's village, and on this road you will meet a tall and handsome woman. She is the mother of the chief."

The little king continued, "This woman will make much of you and will treat you as her own son. She will take you to her home and feed you, and she will dress you in fine clothes. You must repay her with the love and trust that her son has denied her all his life. She will soon grant your every wish."

"And then?" asked the boy.

"When you have gained her confidence, ask for the magic bow and the arrow that flies faster than the wind. She will give them to you. She has kept these since her husband died many years ago, and the son has searched for them in vain. When the bow and arrow are in your possession, take them to the chief. He will give you anything you may ask in exchange. But this time remember not to part with them until the bird is safely in your hands."

All came to pass as the little king had predicted. The boy met the chief's beautiful mother, who took him home with her and treated him as her own son. She lavished both love and gifts upon him. He soon gained her confidence, and she gave him the magic bow and arrow.

The young man took these treasures to her son, the chief. He was careful, however, not to part with either the bow or arrow until the bird was in his hands.

All this made the great chief happy, for now he possessed the two greatest treasures in the kingdom, both of which had been kept from him since his father's death. He willingly parted with his magic bird.

The youth was also happy, for his long, long search was over, and he had carried out his father's wish.

The younger son now made preparations to return to his father's faraway kingdom. But the chief's mother had come to love him so dearly that she promised him in marriage to her favorite daughter. She begged the young man to live with them forever. His life would surely be happy.

The little dwarfs, too, had come to love him, and they were stricken with sorrow at the thought of losing him. They loved him so much, in fact, that their king paid him the honor of adopting him. So now the young man had two fathers.

Torn between two homes, the boy decided to return to his own country and bring back his father to the home of his adoption. Eventually this came to pass when, with a large retinue of servants and many choice gifts for his people, the youth set forth upon his journey.

All went well until the young man reached his brother's village. Here he found both his brother and his followers in a sorry state. They were without food and ill. Many of them had died, and quarrels had broken out, each blaming the others for their plight. And also, they were homesick for their people.

"Come," said the younger to the elder brother kindly, "I will take you and your companions back to your homes. You shall rule there in our father's place while he returns with me to the land of my adoption. He shall end his days with me in happiness and comfort."

And so it came about that the younger son's singleness of purpose reaped a rich reward, not only for himself, but for the brother who had wronged him. Both benefited to the end of their days.

The old father found great happiness in his

younger son's new home. There his grandchildren and great-grandchildren played around him as he whiled away the days of his extreme old age in the sunshine.

The bird with the golden legs was also a constant pleasure to the old man, for its song proved to be as beautiful as its plumage. Once in his possession, the bird obeyed the old man's every wish—even to supplying his daily needs.

This Ngoni story from Malawi is attributed by Phyllis Savory to R. A. M. Year as narrator. It appears in *Fireside Tales from the North.*

Tales Told by the Zulu People

The Tortoise and His Boast

THE RAINS WERE VERY LATE, AND THE WHOLE countryside was parched and dry. The cattle were hollow-eyed and thin, as they licked the mud for the only moisture left in the riverbed.

"The spirit of the river is angry," the old men muttered among themselves. "Maybe a gift would bring forth water for our beasts and ourselves to drink."

Dinga, the little herd boy, listened to their talk. At noon the following day, as his cattle licked the mud, Dinga said, "O River, the best black ox in my father's herd I bring to you today. He is yours if you will let the water rise up for all to drink."

But no water came, and the thirsty beasts mooed in despair.

"Maybe," Dinga continued, "a red bull would please you more? Here is one, the best in all the land. Take him and fill the pool for all to drink."

Still the water refused to come.

Now there was one among the herd, a milk-white flawless cow, Dinga knew to be the pride of his father's heart. This cow the boy drove forward from the rest.

"Take Mhlope, and my father's heart goes with her—only let the water come!" pleaded Dinga.

But the cracks in the hard, dry riverbed seemed to widen and smile, refusing his bribe.

In despair, Dinga searched his mind for something that would please. Then he said to the river, "I have a little sister at my father's house. A laughing, fat, and happy child. Even *her* will I give to you if you will quench the thirst of all!"

As the words left his lips, the water bubbled up, crystal clear, and filled the pool for all to drink.

After a time, Dinga went home to fetch his little sister, Nompofo. He told her they would play beneath the trees that fringed the riverbank.

This they did until Nompofo fell asleep, her

cheek resting on her little hands. Then Dinga stole away, leaving her in fulfillment of his promise to the river.

Soon Nompofo awoke, and as she did, the spirit of the river rose up out of the water to claim the girl as his reward.

Nompofo was terrified at the sight of one so strange. Her scream echoed through the hills, as she ran as fast as her fat little legs could carry her, and in time, she escaped.

The girl wandered on and on among the hills, but could not find her home. Finally, as night approached, a well-kept field of mabele, or Kafir corn, came in sight.

"Ah," she thought, "someone must live here!" But she was wrong, for she had wandered far from her own chief's land into the next kingdom. There, animals lived and ruled. The field she came to belonged to King Ndlovu, the elephant.

By this time, Nompofo was very hungry. She made herself a little shelter in a thicket and went to gather some ripe grain. She crushed this between two flat stones, made a fire, and prepared her meal. Then covering herself with branches and grass, she went to sleep.

Early next morning, Nompofo heard talking and laughter nearby. Peeping from her little shelter, she saw the elephant's animal servants collecting the ripe Kafir corn for their king.

Soon she heard one say, "Alert, alert! There is danger close at hand. Can you not smell a foreign smell?" And they all put their noses in the air and sniffed.

Then another one exclaimed, "A thief has stolen our lord Ndlovu's grain. See where the ripened plant has been torn down!"

And they all stamped their feet and turned this way and that. But nowhere could they see the thief.

Now, as the animals neared the thicket where Nompofo hid, she blew her smouldering fire to a blaze, and set the mabele field afire to drive the beasts away.

In panic, they all raced ahead of the flames to report to Ndlovu, calling out, "My lord, my lord, a thief is in your fields!" and "My lord, my lord, your lands are all ablaze!"

The elephant was angered by being disturbed at such an early hour, especially when he saw his servants had come empty-handed from the lands.

The elephant king called the jackal to him and

said, "Go, you who sing to the moon, and kill this creature that has dared to spoil my lands."

So Mpungushe, the jackal, bushy tail dragging on the ground, and nervously looking over his shoulder from time to time, returned to the field.

There he poked his sharp nose first into one bush and then into another, until he finally came to the thicket where Nompofo hid.

"I am Mpungushe," he called out nervously, "the bold and cunning Mpungushe. Come out and let me kill you!"

But Nompofo, making her voice as deep and fierce as she could, replied, "How should I fear one as small as you? I am Nompofo! It is well known that my horns are branched like a tree, with ten sharp points to run you through. Ten creatures such as you would fit comfortably in my mouth. Be ready, for I am coming out!"

The jackal gave a piercing yell and, with his bushy tail between his legs, bolted back to Ndlovu's hut without once looking back.

"My lord, my lord!" he cried. "A wicked giant is in your land. I saw him. He is taller than the trees. Even you he could crush beneath his foot."

There was silence among the animals while the

elephant flapped his great ears backward and forward in distress.

At last one animal spoke. "It would take more than a giant to crush me," boasted Fudu, the tortoise. "I will rid you of your enemy!" And he swaggered down the path toward the field while all the animals craned their necks to watch.

Now, Nompofo was really very frightened and near to tears. She heard Fudu thudding along the path toward her, making all the clatter he could with his heavy shell and singing loudly, "I am the son of my father, I am the son of my father!"

She could hide her fear no longer. Bursting from her hiding place, Nompofo ran screaming into the forest.

Fudu, the tortoise, sat for a long time in the pathway and laughed and laughed and laughed!

At last, he thought, Mpungushe had shown himself in his true colors—the coward of the veld, frightened by a little child who had lost her way! But Fudu decided to keep this part to himself. He was not going to belittle his own daring.

He waddled back to Ndlovu with his thumbs stuck under his armpits. He was still singing loudly, "I am the son of my father! The mighty giant has fled at the sight of the brave and bold Fudu! I am the son of my father."

There was great rejoicing in the kingdom of Ndlovu at Fudu's victory over such a dangerous enemy. In his gratitude, the elephant made the tortoise his chief counselor, while Mpungushe, the jackal, was banished from the land for his cowardice.

Since his downfall the jackal has never had the courage to hunt for himself, but follows the lion, eating the scraps he leaves—and crying to the moon.

This story is titled "The Son of Tortoise" in *Zulu Fireside Tales,* published by Howard Timmins in Cape Town, 1961.

The Song of the Doves

SOMAKHEHLA'S HEART WAS FULL OF SORROW, FOR Nombakatholi, his much loved wife,was without children. It seemed that he would go childless to his grave. Who could have a light heart with such a thought to dog his footsteps?

Nombakatholi loved Somakhehla with all her heart, and her failure to bear him children brought great unhappiness to her. Nightly she cried herself to sleep in the solitude of her hut.

The crops, however, had to be planted, for the rains had commenced. The red-breasted cuckoo called without stopping for the wife to till the fields, and so she took up her hoe and set about her task with a heavy heart.

The sun was shining brightly after the rain, and all the birds, and not just the cuckoo, were singing.

There was so much happiness around her that Nombakatholi in despair beat her head with her hands. She cried out to two doves flying overhead, making the morning sweet with their gentle cooing, "Oh, why should I alone be sad today?"

To her great surprise, the doves answered, saying, "Any why *are* you sad?"

"It is because I have no child to bring laughter to my lord and me," she replied.

"Mfune! Mfune! Mfune!" the doves chanted as they dropped from above and took places on either side of her.

"Make a bed within the earthen pot that stands against the wall," they cooed.

As the wife did as the doves had commanded, there was a chorus of "Mfune! Mfune!" from the trees around the hut. Surely all the doves in the world had gathered to add their songs of praise to those of the two beside her.

"Cover the pot with care and do not look within until the moon has gone to rest," chanted the doves, and their friends once more took up the song.

When she had followed their instruction, the

wife took the doves from the dimness of the hut into the beautiful sunshine of the spring morning. As the two doves rose into the air, they called back to her, "Watch your pot, and tell no one of what has passed today until the time is ready. Mfune! Mfune!"

As the gray dawn broke on the following day, Nombakatholi lifted the lid of her big grain pot and looked inside. A sob of joy came from her lips as she saw, lying on the little goatskin bed, the dimpled body of a baby girl.

The little one stretched up her arms, and for the first time in many months, Nombakatholi's joyous laughter filled the hut.

She called the baby Fihliwe, which means the hidden one. As the years passed, the child grew apace both in beauty and kindliness, and her mother kept her secret safe from all.

When Nombakatholi worked by day, she hid little Fihliwe in the big grain pot. She put special marks of sorrow around her hut so that none would enter there.

Somakhehla, her husband, was puzzled from time to time at voices coming from the hut at night when Nombakatholi and her daughter played. Sometimes he thought there was the sound as though a baby cried. He asked his wife what caused these sounds.

"Ah, my lord," she sighed. "I often talk with myself at the sorrow that is mine, that I should have no children. Sometimes, too, I cry." Knowing the ways of women, Somakhehla was satisfied.

As Fihliwe grew in beauty and in years, so she grew in grace. When she had reached the marriage age, she was lovelier than any maiden in the land.

Nombakatholi felt that the time had come to make her secret known. She therefore dressed Fihliwe in the gayest beads, while in her hair she twined flowers from the forest. Then she sent the girl to the water hole to draw water to cook the midday meal.

Now, the great Mveli, much loved chief of all the land, was standing by the water hole to watch his royal cattle quench their thirsts. Fihliwe, with downcast eyes and water pot upon her head, passed.

The girl raised her eyes and, as his gaze met hers, the great chief's heart stood still. Such beauty he had never seen, and he was speechless as he looked upon her sweetness.

At last he found his voice and said, "My pretty one, your face is strange to me. Do you come from far afield and whom do you visit here?"

"I am Somakhehla's daughter," Fihliwe said, shyly looking down.

"But that cannot be," Mveli said. "Somakhehla is a childless man. Come, child, tell me your name."

"I know no other hut than that of Nombakatholi, Somakhehla's wife," she insisted. And a gentle cooing filled the air as her guardian doves circled around her head as she took the pathway to her home.

Mveli stood as though he had been turned to stone. Then when he had found his voice once more, he called his headman to him.

"Follow that maiden to her father's huts," he ordered. "I would have her as my foremost wife."

Therefore when the headman saw Fihliwe enter Nombakatholi's hut, he took the news to Mveli.

"Prepare a fitting gift and take it to the father of the girl," said the chief, "and let him know my wish."

Carrying Mveli's gift in his hand, the headman went to the village council tree, and there he gave Mveli's message to Somakhehla.

"I am a man of sorrow," said the old man, beating his hands upon his chest. "I have no child to bring blessings to me in my old age nor to fulfill the wishes of your lord."

It was then that Nombakatholi called her husband to her and told him the strange story of the
kindness of the doves and how the birds' magic had
given them their child. Then she brought Fihliwe
out for him to see.

The father, too, was left speechless and held his
hands before his eyes as though her beauty blinded
him. In his joy he turned to those near him and said,
"Tonight we feast! Kill my fattest cow and let the
preparations be made." Then turning to Mveli's headman, he said, "I gladly give Fihliwe to your lord."

Now as Nombakatholi heard her husband's
words, she brought out her roll of woven mats. These
she unrolled from the doorway of her hut right down
the pathway that led to the council tree where
Mveli's headman sat. She bade Fihliwe walk with
pride along this path for all to see—a fitting bride for
Mveli's royal kraal.

This story is from *Zulu Fireside Tales*. The author gives the
following respellings to aid in the pronunciation of names:
Somakhehla, som-ke-slah; Nombakathole, nom-bah-kah-taw-
le; mfune, mfoo-ne; Fihliwe, fee-slee-we.

Tales Told by the Xhosa People

The Moon Girl

THANGALIMLIBO WAS THE DAUGHTER OF A VERY
poor man named Lungelo. He was indeed so poor
that his only possession besides his lovely daughter
was a solitary cow which supplied the two with milk.

Thanga, as her father fondly called her, was
given her name when she was left motherless shortly
after birth. Her father had called her 'The Little
Pumpkin Without a Stem.'

For a short while, her grandmother had cared
for the newborn baby. But her father soon took
Thanga to his lonely hut in the hills. There she could
grow up to early womanhood under his loving care.

But the little one was always far from being an ordinary child. From her earliest babyhood, she refused to sleep at nighttime, preferring to sing and dance all through the silent hours. She was at her happiest playing or working in the moonlight.

Thanga's father indulged her in this whim because of what her mother had said just before death: "Lungelo, my husband, you must never take our little one into the sunlight. If you should do so, you will lose her forever." After saying these words, the mother closed her eyes in peace.

Lungelo always carefully followed his dead wife's instruction in this, and little Thanga grew to be a beautiful girl, so beautiful that her fame spread far afield.

Not only was the girl famed for her lovely looks but for the fine crops she raised by her hard work in the hours when other folk rested. Thanga tended her aging father's fields while the moon shed its pale light over the sleeping countryside.

The few who saw the girl spread the fame of her beauty abroad until everyone longed to see the Moon Girl, Thangalimlibo.

The only son of a faraway chief heard of this wonder girl and felt that, come what may, he must know for himself the truth of these reports. Could they possibly be true?

"Surely one of such beauty and diligence combined," he thought, "would be a fitting bride for the heir to a chieftainship as great as that of my father."

The young man dressed himself in his best visiting attire and set out for Thanga's home. But realizing that he had little hope of seeing her by daylight, the chief's son waited at the spring where she nightly drew the water for her father's hut.

As the full moon climbed into a cloudless sky, the girl came singing happily down the path. She, too, was dressed in her best attire and her lovely body shone brightly in the moonlight. Her beads and bracelets glittered like precious stones set in silver as they caught the moonbeams. Her face was bright as the moon itself and her teeth were white as she smiled shyly to greet the good-looking stranger at the spring.

The boy caught his breath as she paused, not knowing what to say. Thanga's heart was beating as fast as the young man's, and no words were needed between them.

The next step in the courtship was to ask the maiden's father for permission for the young people to meet. This the chief's son lost no time in doing, and seeing their radiant faces, Lungelo willingly gave his consent.

The chief's son went home with a happy heart to tell his father of his good fortune and the beauty of his chosen bride.

The chief, however, had heard of Thanga's strange behavior. He was anything but pleased to think he would have a daughter-in-law who spent her daylight hours in sleeping. But nothing other than marriage would satisfy the boy. His mother realized his determination, and she persuaded her husband to speak to Thanga's father about the betrothal.

Before long, everything was settled. After a large price for the bride had been paid, a moonlight wedding was arranged.

Thanga's father had a warning for the bridegroom. He was never to let his bride go out into the sunshine. If she did so, a great tragedy would befall him and the young man would lose his bride forever.

Life passed happily for Thanga and her husband in her new home. Thanga soon gained her mother-in-law's respect and affection for her diligence at night.

"What matters it," the old woman said to her chief, "if I gather the wood for the hut instead of our daughter? I am young at heart and strong. Think of the work she does in our fields at nighttime. I tell you, we are fortunate in our son's choice."

In the face of such praise, the chief was forced to hold his tongue although Thanga's strange ways constantly annoyed him. He did not believe that the girl would vanish if she went out into the sunlight.

All went well for a time, and a strong, healthy son was born to Thanga. They named the baby boy Dantalasele.

One sunny day, inside the hut, the fat and laughing baby lay in his mother's lap when the chief called to her to fetch some water from the spring.

Thanga looked around helplessly for her husband, hoping he would help her. But he had gone, she remembered, on a journey to a faraway village. She had seen her mother-in-law leave for the fields only a few minutes earlier, hoe over her shoulder. There was no help for Thanga.

"My father," she said humbly to the chief, "may I be allowed to do your bidding when the sun has set?"

The old man would not listen. He told Thanga angrily that he would beat her if she did not carry out his order. So with a heavy heart, Thanga handed the baby to his nursemaid, saying, "Child, care for Dantalasele while I am gone."

Taking up a scoop, Thanga put the water gourd upon her head and went out into the sunshine to follow her father-in-law's command.

At the spring, Thanga looked nervously around her, then dipped the scoop into the water to fill the big gourd. As she did so, the scoop slipped from her hand and dropped into the crystal clear water. Thanga saw it sink down, down, until it was lost to sight.

"Now, how did it slip from my hand like that?" she said to herself.

Trying to find a way to fill the gourd, she took off her head covering and holding the four corners in one hand, she made a bag. She lowered this into the spring to draw up water. But it, too, slipped from her fingers and she watched it follow the scoop out of sight.

"What clumsiness is this that makes my fingers all thumbs today?" she asked anxiously. She took off her leather skirt to make a scoop with that because she knew she had to return with the water. The skirt filled and billowed out in the water. One time should draw up almost enough, Thanga thought. But when she made ready to pull up the skirt, with a swirl and a tug, it escaped her fingers. It went down until it, too, was lost to sight.

"How shall I clothe myself when I go home?" Thanga thought. But first there remained the problem of the gourd to be filled. Maybe she could cover herself with some branches from the trees. She dipped the gourd itself into the water. Completely filled, it would be a heavy weight for her to pull up alone. But if she half filled it, she could manage.

The water began to trickle into the gourd and she was almost ready to pull it up when an unseen force dragged it from her grasp. Thanga bent down lower to catch the gourd as it sank. She groped in the water to save it, but once her hand was below the surface, the water grasped Thanga and would not let her go.

Into the depths of the water the unseen power pulled Thanga, and down, down, down it took her until she reached the home of the spirits of the spring. They bade her welcome, and there they kept her.

As time went on and Thanga did not return, Dantalasele became hungry and began to cry.

The grandfather, the old chief, said to the little nurse, "Child, go and see why the baby's mother is so long at the spring. Bid her feed him, then tell her to hurry home for I am hungry and as yet no food has been cooked. The dark will soon be here."

The nurse put the baby on her back and hurried to the spring. But when she saw no sign of her mistress there, she returned to the chief with the news that only Thanga's footprints were to be seen in the sand at the water's edge.

As time passed, Dantalasele became more and more hungry. Soon the chief began to worry at what he had done. And matters did not improve when his wife came from the fields. She scolded her husband for his stubbornness in going against his son's wishes, and she chided him far into the night.

They tried to feed the baby on curdled milk, but he spat it out and cried all the more. After many hours the baby, his grandparents, and the nurse fell into an exhausted sleep.

But his empty stomach soon wakened little Dantalasele and he started to cry. The little nurse took him outside to comfort him. She walked toward the spring, but all along the path the baby cried. Soon the girl began to sing in a tearful voice,

> Dantalasele is crying,
> The moon is shining,
> The baby is crying.

As her last words died on the stillness of the night, she reached the water's edge. Thanga rose from the depths of the spring. Reaching out her arms, she took the baby to her breast and let him drink his fill. She kept him while the nurse rested, then she returned the baby to the girl and told her to take him home.

"You must not tell those at home where I am," she said, "for the spirits of the underworld have claimed me and they will not let me go."

When morning came, little Dantalasele was laughing and full of happiness once more. His grandparents could not understand the reason, although the nurse assured them that she had satisfied his hunger with water from the spring.

Each night after that, while the old people slept, and in the daytime, too, when she went to fetch water for the hut, the little nurse took the baby to his mother. As the nurse sang her song, Thanga rose from the water to feed Dantalasele. She played with him before returning to the underworld, and the grandparents continued to wonder at the child's happiness and contentment.

After three days had passed, the husband returned from his visit. The old man bowed his head in shame as he told his son that through his foolishness and disbelief Thanga had disappeared.

Although heartbroken and angry, the husband was relieved to find that at least his baby son was well and happy. But he refused to believe the nurse's story about feeding the baby on the water from the spring. When she crept from the hut that night, he stealthily followed her.

With what amazement and joy the young husband saw Thanga rise from the water in answer to the nurse's sad song. He watched silently as the mother fed their little son. He dared not show himself for fear she would disappear again. So, with a troubled heart, he returned to tell his mother what he had seen.

"Wait until the moon is high tonight, my son," she advised him, "then go to the spring and capture her by force."

When evening came, the young husband tied a length of oxhide thong beneath his arms. He asked his friends to hold the other end and hid with them among the reeds beside the spring.

It was a long wait until the nurse carrying the baby came down the path, singing her sorrowful little song. Thanga rose to the surface as the girl reached the water's edge.

But this time Thanga seemed uneasy and looked around her nervously before she took the child.

"Did no one come with you?" she asked the girl.

At that moment the husband rushed forward and caught Thanga while his friends pulled on the thong with all their strength. Slowly the young man and the struggling woman were pulled along the path. But Thanga was not easily to be rescued. To the fear of everyone, the water, hissing and roaring, began to foam and swirl around them.

Higher and higher the water rose until it seemed that the waves would engulf the very huts themselves.

The mighty force of the waves dragged the man and wife apart, leaving Dantalasele in his father's arms. Thanga disappeared beneath the surface of the water once more.

On the following night when all was still and quiet, the sorrowing husband again went to the spring. He waited, hoping, at the water's edge, calling his wife by name from time to time.

Never a ripple disturbed the surface of the water. At last in despair the young man called loudly upon his ancestors to help him in his trouble.

As if in answer, there emerged from the depths of the water a cock. It was like no earthly bird the man had ever seen, and it shone like the rising sun. What was more, it spoke.

"What disturbs you, young man?" the cock questioned.

The chief's son related his troubles, telling the cock of how, through fear of her father-in-law, Thanga had disobeyed the orders of the underworld that had been laid down for her at her birth. To punish her, the spirits had taken Thanga to live with them at the bottom of the spring.

"All this I understand," the cock said kindly, nodding his head, "and I will help you. You are being punished for your father's foolish act, so your father must bear the costs. Go now, and bring from his herd two fat oxen and a pitch-black bull. Such gifts will please the spirits of the spring and they will restore your wife to you."

The chief's son went home with a happy heart to do the cock's bidding. As the sun sank below the horizon that evening he drove the three cattle to the spring.

The golden cock met him at the water's edge. As the husband urged the two oxen into the water, the strange bird followed, proudly mounted on the big black bull.

There was silence for a long time after this. At last the water parted, and Thangalimlibo appeared, looking more beautiful than she ever looked before. She was clothed in shining beads and garments from the underworld.

Speechless with joy, her husband took her hand, and as the dawn colored the sky around them, they made their way home. Never again would Thanga be asked to go out in the sunshine.

Then one by one, the spring threw up the things it had taken from Thanga: the scoop, the head covering, the skirt, and the big gourd. There Thanga's mother-in-law found them when she went to draw the water in the evening as mists gathered.

Originally titled "The Moon Girl Thangalimlibo" in *Xhosa Fireside Tales,* published by Bailey Bros. & Swinfen in London, 1963. In his Foreword, D. McK. Malcolm notes that Xhosa tales often suggest that hardship if stoically endured is good for individual character.

The Magic Bowl and Spoon

Mᴅɪɴɪɴɪ ᴀɴᴅ ʜɪs ᴡɪꜰᴇ, Nʏᴇɴɢᴜʟᴀ, ᴡᴇʀᴇ ᴠᴇʀʏ poor. But although the husband had to work for their living, they could look back to times when there was no need for such toil, to times when Mdinini's ancestors had ruled this land. Then there had been great flocks and herds.

Now all that was left of this bygone splendor was the ancestral wooden bowl and spoon in which Mdinini's wife daily served his midday meal of amasi, milk curds.

It was a well-known rule throughout the land that such a spoon and bowl were passed from father to son, and from son to son again. Such heirlooms should be used by none but the rightful owner. This was 'The Rule of the Ancestors,' and none dared disobey it.

Having no children to help them in their daily tasks, life was indeed hard for these two. One day Mdinini said to Nyengula, "Wife, there is little to keep starvation from us. I must go and seek work from the rich chief over the hills to earn our living for a while. When my term of service is completed, I will ask for payment in the form of fine young cows, that we may build up a herd once more."

Nyengula nodded, and Mdinini continued, "You must care for our home while I am gone. Whatever comes to pass, *you must not use my ancestral bowl and spoon!* For as you know, I, and only I, may use them."

After Nyengula had assured her husband that she would respect his wishes, he set off on his long journey to the home of the rich chief over the hills. There he found work.

For a time Nyengula faithfully obeyed her husband's orders. She swept their hut, tilled their tiny garden, and kept everything in order ready for his return.

But daily, as she cleaned and tidied all around her, the ancestral wooden bowl and spoon seemed to call and mock her from the wall on which they hung. At first she was afraid even to touch them lest something dreadful should befall her.

But it would never do, she thought, for her husband to find his precious possessions covered with dust on his return. So one day she carefully took down the bowl and spoon and dusted them. Nothing happened. She looked to see if they had marked her hands and was relieved to find no change.

"Just an ordinary old bowl and spoon after all," she thought as she hung them up again.

Day after day, Mdinini's forefathers' possessions continued to tempt and torment Nyengula. And the more she tried to put the matter from her mind, the greater her desire became to eat from the forbidden bowl and spoon.

At last the temptation was too much for Nyengula. She took the bowl and spoon from the peg on which they hung. Instead of returning them after their usual dusting, she placed the spoon inside the bowl, just as she had always done when preparing her husband's food. Then she prepared the good porridge to eat with the amasi, and made ready for her meal.

As Nyengula bent down to place the food in the bowl, she was startled to hear a voice come out of the bowl.

"Nyengula, if you wish to respect your husband's orders, do not put any food in me!"

But by now she had firmly set her mind on carrying out her desire to eat from the forbidden bowl and spoon.

Nyengula answered angrily, "What! you wooden bowl—why should I not use you, when it is my wish to do so? And why should I obey a piece of wood? A human being carved you into what you are, and now you try to give a human being orders! I have never heard of such a thing."

The woman, however, felt slightly uncomfortable when the bowl answered her. "Those who play with fire are apt to get their fingers burned."

But she told the bowl angrily to hold its tongue, if it had one, and turned to lift down the skin bag that held the amasi.

She did hesitate when, as she laid her hand upon the spoon, it said, "Nyengula, I heard your husband reminding you about the customs of this home and warning you not to use us. Now what are you intending to do?"

But Nyengula only laughed and replied, "This is a strange home indeed—a talking bowl and a talking spoon. Whoever heard of such a thing? Hold your tongues, both of you! There is nobody here to see me, so I will sit in the sun and eat amasi in you, bowl, and with you, spoon."

Once more the bowl and spoon warned her. Together this time they said, "Nyengula, for the last time, listen to our words of warning. In this home you know it is against the custom for a woman to sit in the sun and eat her amasi."

But the stubborn woman refused to listen and, taking up the bowl of food, she put the spoon in it and left the hut. She chose a nice sunny place, and sitting down, began her meal.

"Hmm! Wonderful spoons and bowls in this home," she muttered to herself. "They can talk!"

She put the first spoonful of the mixed porridge and amasi into her mouth. Good! She was going to enjoy her forbidden meal in the sunshine.

Then followed a second spoonful. She would teach the bowl and spoon not to call down threats upon her head, indeed she would.

But what happened? As the third spoonful went into her mouth, the spoon stuck firmly. Nothing she could do would loosen it. And the more she tried to pull it out, the farther down her throat it went—until spluttering and crying for mercy, Nyengula sank exhausted to the ground.

"There you are!" laughed the bowl. "The ancestors have got you, as we said they would! You were too clever to be warned by a bowl and a spoon, so now you can find your own way out of your trouble."

The poor woman cried and moaned for help to no avail. At last there came a crow to see what all the noise was about. Not being able to speak, Nyengula pointed to the spoon in her mouth, trying to ask for help. But she got no sympathy from the heartless bird. He only laughed at her distress and flew away, croaking hoarsely, "It serves you right. It serves you right!"

A little later two doves flew by, and hearing her moans, they asked Nyengula what was wrong. Again she pointed to her mouth, and the birds had pity on her.

Understanding her punishment, they asked what they could do to help. Should they call her husband?

She nodded her head vigorously and pointed to the mountains. The little doves flew away.

Before long the birds came to a group of workers hoeing in a field. "Maybe her husband is among them," said one dove to the other.

They perched upon a nearby tree, and together they began to sing,

Nyengula, the wife, disobeyed her husband.
Now she is caught by a wooden spoon.
Mdinini, please come and release her.

But no one took the slightest notice of the birds or their song. So, sorrowfully shaking their heads, the doves continued their search. Time and again they stopped to sing their sad song wherever they saw workers hoeing in a field.

At last the doves came to the place over the hills where Mdinini had been hired.

This time, as they reached the end of the first line of their song, they saw a man put down his hoe to listen. And when he heard the second line, he looked around to see who sang the song.

Seeing the little doves, the man understood their message. He left his work and hurried to his master to ask permission to return to his home. His request was granted.

All night long Mdinini traveled. In the morning he reached home and found his disobedient wife kneeling down by the side of the hut in great distress. Because of the ancestral spoon, her mouth was wide open.

"What ails you, wife?" he asked. But of course she could not tell him. With tears running down her cheeks, Nyengula pointed to her mouth.

"Ah!" exclaimed her husband. "Did I not tell you never to use my ancestral bowl and spoon? See what comes of your willful disobedience? But I will try to save you," he continued, "for otherwise you will surely die."

Reverently Mdinini then called upon the mercy of his ancestors, naming them one by one, and begging their forgiveness of his foolish wife.

When this was done, he grasped the handle of the spoon and pulled it from Nyengula's mouth, saying, "Wife, your disobedience will one day cause your death—as it would have done this time, had it not been for the kindness and mercy of our little friends the doves." And in his gratitude Mdinini scattered grain for the birds.

Never again did Nyengula disobey her husband's wishes, for she had more than learned her lesson. And never again did the bowl or spoon have cause to call down the ancestors' displeasure on any of Mdinini's household.

Originally titled "The Rule of the Ancestors" in *Xhosa Fireside Tales*. A story like this was told to support family discipline and tribal custom, here having to do with ancestor worship.

When the Husband Stayed Home

THERE ARE LAZY PEOPLE IN ALL PARTS OF THE
world, including Xhosaland. In this country there
once lived a man and his wife in a little old hut. They
had a comfortable home that was always neat and
tidy even though it had seen better days.

Their one precious cow was always sleek and
fat, their dogs well cared for, and their hens clucked
contentedly around the yard. Velaphi, their baby
girl, was a joy to one and all.

All this, and a great deal more besides, was the
work of Nomdudo, Mbebe's busy wife. She saw to
the smooth running of the home while Mbebe tilled
their two fields and planted the crops.

But Mbebe himself was as lazy as could be, and there were times when he would let the crops look after themselves. Each morning he put his hoe over his shoulder as usual when he left the house so that his wife would think he was bent on business. But as soon as he was out of sight, he branched off the path to visit his friends.

He would spend the day in idle gossip while the weeds in his fields grew and grew and grew. And when Mbebe returned to Nomdudo at nighttime to find a well-cooked supper awaiting him, he would scold her.

"You lazy woman, don't you *ever* work while I am away seeing to the crops? Where is the sleeping mat to replace my old one? And where is the new beer pot I need?"

On and on he would grumble.

Patient Nomdudo bore these scoldings for a long time. But she could finally no longer endure his unjust and scolding tongue.

One night she said, "Husband, I have listened to your scoldings for the last time. Tomorrow you and I will change places for the day. *I* will do the hoeing, and *you* will take care of the household work."

The next morning Nomdudo took the hoe and set out for the fields.

She called over her shoulder to Mbebe, "Now, husband, please remember these things. First of all, clean the hut and the yard. Velaphi must be fed and cared for. And do not forget that she is young and will need many meals throughout the day. The cow must be milked and grazed, but do not let her stray into our neighbor's fields. The dogs will steal food if you do not satisfy their hunger."

She caught her breath and continued, "The milk must be set for curdling in the bag that hangs on the centerpole in the hut. The firewood is ready, but do not forget that clean water must be carried from the

spring before you cook the evening meal. I shall be hungry when I return and shall look forward to some well-cooked porridge."

Having completed her instructions, Nomdudo left for the fields.

"Well," Mbebe thought, "I have all the day before me for these simple tasks so I can afford to do them at my leisure."

But little Velaphi thought otherwise. She had awakened with a healthy appetite and raised her voice in no uncertain manner.

"Bother the child!" her father thought. But he quickly fed her. Then slinging the baby on his back as Nomdudo did, he tied her tightly to him so that he would have both hands free for the work ahead.

Mbebe swept and cleaned the hut and yard. But the child was tied too tightly, and besides, she missed her mother's songs and her gentle rocking as she worked. The little one made her unhappiness known by constant fussing.

After the yard had been swept, Mbebe began to milk the cow. But the cow resented the unfamiliar hands and missed Nomdudo's kindly voice so much that halfway through she kicked over the wooden bucket and spilled most of the milk.

Mbebe, worried that there was too little milk left for curdling, forgot to feed the cow and left her tied up where she stood. Forgetting the dogs that waited expectantly for food, Mbebe went into the hut and sat down.

"In truth," he said to himself, "this work has made me thirsty. I will pay a quick visit to my brother Malumi's hut and see if his beer is ready. One swallow is all that I need to take the dryness from my tongue. I will soon be back."

But his brother's brew proved to be the best that his sister-in-law had ever made. It was a very long time before Mbebe was able to drag himself back to his household chores.

When he did return to the hut, he found the hungry dogs pulling the bag filled with milk around the yard as they tried to get at the curds inside it.

It was fortunate, however, that the dogs had not found the pail half filled with milk that he had forgotten to put into the bag for curdling. Mbebe drove the dogs away, washed the bag, and filled it with the milk left in the wooden pail.

He turned his attention to the hungry hens that had pecked a large hole in the storage bin and were helping themselves to the grain.

It was now nearly time to prepare the evening meal. Being short of firewood, Mbebe decided to pull some sticks from the stable to make a fire.

This reminded him that the cow was still tied up inside, where he had left her after milking.

Well, he would quickly bring the fresh water from the spring, he decided, and while it was heating on the fire, he would see to some food for the cow.

The hungry dogs, however, were sniffing around the centerpole where the bag of curds hung. Taking little Velaphi from his back, her father tied her to the pole and put the milk bag on his back for safety. He then hurried to the spring for the water.

As Mbebe stooped to draw the water, the rope that held the mouth of the bag closed came loose. Milk poured out all over his shoulder and into the clear water of the spring, turning it a milky color.

The result of the accident was that Mbebe hurried home with the clouded water and an empty milk sack. He set the water to boil, then he thought about the cow. By now the poor animal was hungry indeed, for she had had nothing to eat all day.

"It is too late," he said to himself, "to take her out to graze. I will put her on the roof and let her eat the thatch. It is time Nomdudo renewed it."

Mbebe placed some of the poles from the stable against the hut and, with a great deal of pulling and struggling, managed to persuade the hungry animal onto the roof of the hut.

"I must tie her up somehow," he thought to himself as he put the thong by which she was held down through the thatch near the centerpole that supported the roof. Once back inside the hut, he tied the thong to his own leg to make sure the cow did not stray.

This done, Mbebe settled down with a sigh of relief to cook the evening meal in readiness for Nomdudo's return. As the water in the big pot began to boil, he hummed cheerfully to himself.

"Surely," he thought, "I have got everything right at last."

But at that very moment the cow lost her footing on the sloping roof above. Off she fell, dangling on the end of the thong that had tied her. And to make matters worse, her weight pulled Mbebe to the top of the tall centerpole. There by his leg he hung, unable to free himself.

Nomdudo returned from her hoeing just as the cow was about to strangle as she swung on the end of the thong.

But Nomdudo did not realize that her husband was hanging at the top of the centerpole inside the hut.

When she cut the thong, Mbebe fell into the pot of boiling water and was killed.

"Look," said Nomdudo to those who came to comfort her, "at the result of laziness!"

Originally titled "Mbebe and His Wife" in *Xhosa Fireside Tales*. The husband and wife who change duties is a familiar theme in folklore and here shows how a story can be adapted to the culture of the teller.

The Wonderful Water Pot

MZANYWA WAS THE PROUD OWNER OF A MAGIC earthern water pot, or ingcazi. So precious was this possession that he would allow no one to handle it but himself. And who could blame him? Did it not turn the sparkling water from the spring into mellow beer or to sweetest milk at his wish? Surely a pot with such magical powers was safe in no other hands but his.

However, Vuyile, his first-born daughter, longed more and more as she grew in years to carry water in this magic pot.

"Surely," she thought, "some of its magic will be transferred to me if only I could carry water in it once."

Her chance came one day when her father and mother, Mamasomi, went to a dance at a neighboring village.

"Daughter, fetch some water for me to cook the evening meal when I return," her mother called over her shoulder as she left. "And care for Hluphekile while we are gone." Hluphekile was Vuyile's younger sister—a jealous and naughty little girl six years old.

"Now," said Vuyile to herself when her parents were out of sight, "at last here is a chance for me to carry out my wish. Who is there to stop me? None need ever know, and I shall soon discover what magic powers my father's wonderful ingcazi holds for me!" Placing the precious pot upon her head, she walked toward the river.

Hluphekile hurried along the path behind her sister, trying to keep up with her long strides. But Hluphekile was a fat little girl, and her legs were very short. Soon she was left far behind.

"So she would forget me?" the child muttered angrily to herself as she lost sight of her big sister. "I will teach her not to ignore me as she does!"

Hluphekile gathered a small handful of the tall grass that grew along the edge of the path. She tied it to a similar bunch from the other side of the path, making a good strong knot.

The little sister smiled to herself as she thought how this trick, played by so many generations of children, would trip her sister.

But one trap was not enough. Sometimes the person using the path might safely step over a single trap. Hluphekile must make more.

She ran a short way farther along the path after her sister, then tied two more bunches of grass together. And farther on she tied still another two. The girl hugged her small shoulders with delight as she sat down at the side of the path to watch the result of her mischief.

She did not have long to wait before Vuyile, her eyes looking straight in front of her to balance the precious water pot upon her head came striding back along the path.

Catching her toe in the first trap, Vuyile stumbled. But with great presence of mind she recovered herself and grasped the pot in time to save it from crashing to the ground.

"Ech!" she exclaimed, not seeing her sister hiding behind some bushes. "A thousand plagues on those naughty herd boys! Wait until I discover who has tricked me in this manner," and with a good-natured laugh she continued on her way.

With the grass brushing her knees and almost hiding the pathway, she hurried on. It was impossible for her to see the second trap, and once more she caught her foot. This time she landed on her knees. But by some miracle she saved the pot again.

Vuyile looked around her in anger for the little

herd boys whom she still blamed for the trick. Seeing no one, she decided to hurry home and leave the water there before returning to punish the naughty boys.

After a short rest, Vuyile continued homeward, carefully watching the path for further pranks.

But the last trap was too well concealed for her to see, and balancing the heavy pot upon her head made it difficult for Vuyile to examine the path closely.

Catching her foot in the trap, she fell down. This time there was a sickening crash, and her father's precious magic ingcazi lay shattered in a dozen fragments on the ground.

"Oh!" she cried, horrified at what she saw. "My father's magic pot! Whatever shall I do?"

Too frightened of her father's anger to return home, Vuyile sat weeping at the side of the path.

Soon her little sister caught up with her. Laughing at the broken pot, she said, "Our father will thrash you when he knows what you have done," and she went on her way alone.

In the evening when the girls' parents returned to their hut they found Hluphekile there alone. They asked where her older sister was.

"Oh," answered Hluphekile, "she broke her father's magic pot and is afraid to return to her home."

"What is a pot, although it is a magic one," exclaimed the father, "next to my own flesh and blood? Go, Hluphekile, and bring your sister home. The hut is lonely without her happiness and laughter."

Out into the night the younger sister went and soon found Vuyile, cold and weeping, under the shelter of some bushes by the path.

But the little sister had not come to the end of her mischief. Besides being a naughty girl, she was very jealous of her older sister's easy, laughing good nature. She imagined her parents loved their older daughter more than their younger one. She therefore decided to follow up her mischief with deceit.

"I come from our father with this message," she said. "He commands, 'Go, never again do I wish to set eyes on the one who broke my magic pot.'"

With all hope for forgiveness gone, Vuyile wandered cold and miserable into the night. And Hluphekile went home to tell her parents that she had searched for her sister in vain.

All through the night Vuyile tramped the countryside, until she was completely lost.

Day after day, she searched for some village or hut without success. She lived on the fruits and roots she found growing by the wayside.

Vuyile was in sad condition when one night she saw a light that twinkled in the distance. She hurried toward it, hoping to find food and shelter at last.

When the girl reached the hut from which the light came, she found several people sitting around a bright fire. As she stood timidly at the open door, a voice inside said, "Night is no time for one as young and beautiful as you to be wandering abroad. Child, from where do you come, and why are you alone?"

Sadly Vuyile told the tale of the broken pot and of how, having been turned away from her home by her father's words, she had wandered in the wilds.

"Come in," said the good-looking owner of the voice as he came to the doorway. "All this land belongs to me, and, as chief, I bid you welcome to my kraal."

On the following morning the man sent for Vuyile and said, "My child, you are homeless and disowned. For a long time now I have searched for someone who can turn this heap of rubble into much needed iron. My warriors are sadly short of spears, and my blacksmiths' anvils have been forced to silence for lack of it. Do this for me, and I will make you my foremost wife."

He pointed to a large mound of broken stone beside him.

"Ah," Vuyile thought. "Perhaps the magic of my father's pot has transferred itself to me." Picking up the two grinding stones nearby as the chief turned away, she took a piece of the rubble, and hoping for success, she started to crush it.

But try as she would, no iron appeared. She was just about to bury her face in her hands to quiet her sobs of disappointment when a little tikoloshe, or gnome, passed by.

Stopped by her sobs, he came up to Vuyile. Putting his skinny hand on her shoulder, he said, "Little one, why are you sad?"

"I am homeless," she sobbed, "and unless by magic I can turn this rubble into iron for the chief who rules this land, I can find no shelter for my head."

She told the gnome all that had befallen her and of the chief's promise to make her his foremost wife if she could carry out his wish.

The tikoloshe was a scheming little creature, as are most of his kind. "Now this," he thought, "is my chance to obtain a well-born human child to bring up as my slave. When the infant has learned my tricks, I will use him for my magic works!"

He whispered in Vuyile's ear, "If I should do your task for you, what will you give me in return?" The gnome waited with a smile for her answer.

To become the wife of such a handsome and powerful chief was indeed a temptation to the homeless girl. She replied without hesitation, "I will give you what you ask."

Without another word, the tikoloshe took the grinding stones from her and bent to his task. For a while he worked in silence, stopping from time to time to throw the iron onto the pile rising in front of him.

"My reward," he said at length, "will be your first-born son. There," he continued, tossing the last of the iron to join the rest, "your son is bound to me. When he has passed his second year, I will come and beckon from the doorway of your hut. Then you must fulfill your pledge." And the gnome went on his way.

The girl's heart beat with excitement, but she quietly sat and waited. The custom in this land did not allow her to hurry to the chief, as she wished to do, to claim the reward she had won. Instead, she waited humbly.

Before long the chief came. Unbelieving, he stood as if rooted to the ground. "Child!" he cried excitedly, "do my eyes trick me?" He bent down and ran his hands over the iron pile before he would believe it was real.

There was merrymaking and feasting when the marriage took place, and cattle were sent to Vuyile's father, who came over the hills to bless her.

As the foremost lady in the land, the bride settled down happily in her new home. When a little son was born to her, she had no thought except for the joys of motherhood.

But as the first year and then the second one crept past, an icy fear laid its fingers on her heart as Vuyile remembered her promise to the little tikoloshe.

The little gnome had not forgotten. He called his people to him and said, "Today I shall go to claim my human child, but all may not go well. The magic of her father's broken ingcazi still remains, and its powers may be too strong for me. Watch my hut. Should it burst into flames while I am gone, then mourn me as dead."

After he had said these words, he set off toward Vuyile's home.

He found the girl, sitting in her hut, with the baby on her lap. A strange feeling made her turn her head toward the open door. There, leaning boldly against the timbers, stood the tikoloshe. He raised his hand and beckoned to her.

At first Vuyile turned her back to him, refusing to notice him or recognize his beckoning hand.

So the gnome went inside the hut and, grasping Vuyile by the shoulder with his skinny fingers, turned her to him. He pointed to the lovely child upon her lap.

"Ah," she cried, "you cannot take him from me. Cut out my heart instead, but leave my child to me!"

"What!" screamed the tikoloshe. "Would you bargain with me?" and he tried to snatch the baby from Vuyile. But she was both tall and strong, so she held the little one above her head, where the gnome could not reach.

Angrier and angrier grew the tikoloshe at being thwarted, until in exasperation he began to choke.

Suddenly the gnome shrieked and Vuyile saw a jagged piece of pottery hurtle through the air toward him. Straight for the little creature's head it flew, hitting him on the temple. He fell groaning to the ground.

Vuyile watched fascinated as the gnome lay twitching at her feet, but soon all movement ceased and she knew that he was dead. She picked up the gnome, to hide it from her husband so he would never know her secret. As she did so, she saw lying where the tikoloshe had fallen a piece of broken ingcazi with a familiar pattern.

Then Vuyile realized that her father's magic pot had made amends for all trouble it had brought her. At the same moment, in the land where the gnome had lived, the people watched the tikoloshe's hut burst into flames, and they knew that they would see him no more.

Originally titled "The Magic Water Pot" in *Xhosa Fireside Tales*. Elements of the European folktale of Rumpelstiltskin are found in this story, along with the Xhosa belief in magic, witches, and wizards. The author believes that on occasion a tale told by a European or American long ago became altered to fit the Bantu way of thinking and eventually entered the folklore of the people.

What the Fish Promised

MAZWI AND HIS WIFE LIVED NEAR THE BANKS OF A
big river that flowed into the sea only a few miles
away.

Although they were poor, life passed happily
enough for them, and the new planting season
seemed to promise good rains for their crops. Their
small plot of land was bright with hope in the sunshine as Mazwi and his young wife came along the
path to the place where they planned to turn over
the red earth for planting.

Mazwi carried some food for the midday meal,
while his wife shouldered a hoe. Their tiny baby was

strapped straddle-legged across his mother's back. He nodded his sleepy head as he was rocked by the motion of her stride.

There was very little shade in the neighborhood of their field, so the mother made a tent with her goatskin robe and a few sticks. There the baby, little Mphephethwa, could lie protected from the sun while his parents worked.

On this particular day, the baby, made drowsy by the golden sunshine, fell into a deep sleep. Presently overhead there flew from the ocean nearby a large sea gull and his mate.

"What strange object is that?" one gull asked the other, pointing with its beak in the direction of the little tent. "Let us alight and find out!" The birds sailed silently down to the ground beside the tent.

Heads first on one side and then on the other, the birds drew nearer and nearer until, gaining courage, they at last looked inside.

"How fat and round," they said to each other, "and surely good to eat. Let us take it home to our children."

Between them, the gulls lifted the sleeping baby and flew with him toward their nest near the seashore.

As the birds rose high into the sky, the baby now was awakened by such rough treatment. Seeing the earth so far beneath him, he began to scream and struggle with all his might.

This was more than the big birds had expected and certainly more than they could deal with. They hastily bore the baby down to the seashore, where terrified by the noise he made, they left him to the mercy of the rising tide.

In the field, the wife rested leaning on her hoe. "My husband," she said to Mazwi, "is that not our son I hear crying so bitterly in the distance? Has he been stolen from us while we worked?"

"Woman, get on with your hoeing," her husband scolded her. "Those cries come from the village across the river," and he pointed in the direction the birds had taken.

With a sigh of resignation his wife bent to her work once more. But she could not forget those terrified screams. As soon as she had finished her hoeing, she hurried to the little shelter she had made.

Sad, indeed, were the parents when they realized they had been robbed of their little son. The weeping mother reproached her grief-stricken husband all along the pathway to their home.

Down on the shore where the baby lay, the waves lapped higher and higher as the tide rose, until finally they reached his fat little body.

Just as this happened, a big fish heard the child's pathetic cries and swam up on a wave to where he lay.

"Come, little one," the fish said kindly. "I will take you to your mother."

Opening its big mouth, the fish swallowed the child, and turning along the coast, it swam quickly in the direction of the baby's home.

Eventually the fish came to a river that emptied into the sea. Swimming up the river, the fish soon reached the bank near which Mazwi and his wife lived. Here the big fish put its head out of the water. Seeing a man about to cross to the opposite bank, the fish sang out in a high-pitched voice,

> I bring you sweet news, O man!
> For I carry a baby boy, O man!
> The sea gulls stole him, O man!
> But I must ask for a reward, O man,
> Because one day he will be rich, O man!

The man looked around him in astonishment because no one was in sight. He was about to continue on his way when the fish brought forth from its mouth the baby boy.

The man stared, for surely this must be the very child who had been lost and for whom his parents searched so feverishly.

With a shout of joy, the man took the baby in his arms, and said to the fish, "Pray, good fish, wait here while I call the child's parents that they may reward you for your kindness."

But poor Mazwi was in trouble. He was overjoyed at the return of his son, but having no possessions, he had no reward to give. He went to the water's edge, prepared to pledge his life if need be to the one who had saved his son.

The fish, however, brushed Mazwi's thanks aside, saying, "Do not worry, human. I saved your son with the knowledge that you are poor. The boy himself will reward me later on, for when he reaches manhood he will indeed be rich. All that I ask of you now is that you will remind him from time to time of the fish who saved his life."

Mazwi was delighted to learn from the fish that his son would gain riches, for he had little to offer the child. So he thanked the good fish once more for its kindness and returned to his wife.

She, of course, was overjoyed not only at the return of her little one, but also at the thought of his wealthy future promised by the fish.

Because he had been returned to them from the very jaws of death, Mphephethwa was even more precious than before to his parents. His every wish was granted; his every whim indulged as they assured him of his wealth to come.

"Why should I work and toil," Mphephethwa would ask from time to time, "when my ancestors have wealth in store for me?"

And before many years had passed, the boy became a lazy good-for-nothing youth who refused to raise a finger to help his hardworking parents.

Matters became worse when his father died. His mother had many quarrels with her proud and foolish son.

When Mphephethwa was eighteen years of age, his mother felt that she could deal with him no longer. She sent for her brother to come and punish the boy for his disobedience and refusal to listen to her words.

"Come," said the uncle when he had lectured the youth on his duty as a son, "there is work for you to do. The time has passed that you should live in idleness. Today we will hunt on the mountaintop."

The mother prepared some corn for their journey, and the two set off up the steep mountain.

The boy knew he must obey his uncle's command. The path they took was rough and often blocked by jagged rocks. The way was not easy.

It was a long and strenuous climb. But at last, weary and aching in every limb, Mphephethwa, at his uncle's side, reached the summit.

Before them was a huge boulder, decorated with many figures carved upon it.

The uncle paused to take a strangely braided bracelet of grass from his arm. He mumbled some strange words, took the boy's right hand, and drew the bracelet over it.

Then, while the uncle muttered some more strange words, the big boulder moved aside to uncover a gaping hole.

"Now, nephew," said the uncle, "the time has come for you to play the part that your ancestors have prepared for you. Listen carefully to what I say, for if you miss one single word of my instructions, you will most certainly meet your end."

As the boy listened, his uncle continued, "First and foremost, climb down into this hole. In the cave

below you will find three earthen pots placed upside
down. Now, starting with the first and smallest, you
must carefully turn them the right way up. What you
will do after this is up to you. But should trouble
meet you, rub your magic bracelet and any problem
will be solved."

The uncle looked at the boy and then said,
"Take all that will be of use to you. Then rub the
bracelet again, and the boulder will return to its
place above the hole. May good fortune attend you,
my sister's son, for I must now leave you to your own
devices."

After making sure that Mphephethwa understood his instructions, the uncle turned and left the
boy standing on the rim of the big dark hole.

It was a great test for this pampered boy, but
Mphephethwa bravely carried out his uncle's orders.
Descending into the cavern, he found the earthen
pots exactly as his uncle described them—placed
upside down and half buried in the dust of ages.

The pot nearest the boy was also the smallest,
and Mphephethwa lost no time in turning it the right
way up.

Imagine his delight when out of it there scrambled many cocks and hens. But the boy's joy was soon

checked. Last of all, there came from the pot a fierce black dog which bared its fangs and made ready to attack him.

Fortunately Mphephethwa still held the heavy stick with which he had left home, and after a short battle he succeeded in killing the creature.

From the first pot, he passed to the second. This one was a great deal larger and was so firmly embedded in the ground that it took all his strength to move it. At last he succeeded and, as he turned it right side up, there was a clatter of little hoofs. Out scampered flocks of sheep and goats, all bleating with joy at their release.

But this time Mphephethwa had to face an even greater danger than before. Last of all, out jumped a great and savage dog. It lost no time attacking and trying to tear the boy limb from limb.

It was a bitter fight that followed, and more than once the big dog nearly pulled the boy down. But Mphephethwa fought bravely and finally beat the great brute to the ground, where he killed it.

He sat for a while to regain his breath. Then he went on to the third and last pot. It was the largest of them all.

Mphephethwa had to work hard to loosen the

pot from the earth in which it was half buried. Great strength was required to turn this pot the right way up. But his work proved worth the effort, for out jumped herds of the finest cattle Mphephethwa had ever seen.

Each herd was a different color—black, white, red, and speckled. Last of all there sprang out their guardian, the largest and most savage dog the boy could ever have imagined.

Like those before it, this dog bared its yellow fangs and made ready to attack him. But Mphephethwa knew that however bravely he fought, he could not hope to overcome such a fierce and enormous creature.

Fortunately, and just in time, the boy remembered his uncle's last piece of advice. He hastily rubbed the magic bracelet. At once the dog ceased its attack and advanced to lie down at the boy's feet, where Mphephethwa killed it.

With all three dangers overcome, Mphephethwa looked at his possessions with pride. How, though, could he get them out of their underground prison, he wondered. Again he rubbed the magic talisman, and again he was not disappointed. The cattle, sheep, goats, and fowls all scrambled back into their

own pots. These pots, he found, were now so light
that he could easily pick up even the largest. Quickly
the boy carried the pots without effort onto the
mountainside.

The boy rubbed his magic bracelet, and the big
round stone rolled back into its old position, blocking
up forevermore the entrance to the cave.

With the biggest pot balanced safely on his
head, and a smaller one under each arm, he began
the struggle down the steep and slippery path, taking
care not to drop his precious load.

It was a difficult undertaking, but he reached
his home without accident and much to his mother's
relief. Her son had been away a long time, and she
feared that ill fortune had befallen him.

Putting down the three pots as he reached his
mother's hut, the boy rubbed his magic bracelet for
the last time. To exclamations of surprise from all
the villagers, the fowls and animals poured out as
before. But this time there were no big dogs to fear.

Now the community was rich indeed, and there
was dancing and singing far into the night.

The following day, four of the fattest oxen were
killed to provide a feast of thanksgiving to the ancestors who had provided the boy with so many gifts.

As the boy's mother dipped her gourd into the river to draw water for the cooking, a big fish raised its head from the water and said to her, "Woman, the time has now come that I should have my reward for restoring your baby son to you eighteen long years ago."

The woman had almost forgotten the part the fish had played in the prophesy of her son's wealth. But being reminded, she asked, "Kind friend, what reward do you wish?"

"My needs are few," replied the fish, "and easily satisfied. All I ask your son to give me is ten each of his newly found possessions."

The mother hurried home to remind her son of the fish's kindness in the past. Not only had the fish saved the boy's life, but it had pressed no claims against his poor father.

Realizing how large a debt he owed, the boy at once doubled the requirements of the fish and drove the animals to the river. There the strange creature accepted them with gratitude.

From this time on, the spoiled boy of old became a respected leader of his people. He built a beautiful village for his many followers. His cattle thrived and multiplied.

When the time came for Mphephethwa's marriage, his mother chose the most beautiful as well as the most diligent wife in all the land to share his wealth with him.

And after living for many years to see her grandchildren playing at her hearth, the old mother died and joined her forefathers—content in the knowledge of her son's position and his happiness.

Originally titled "The Story of Mphephethwa" in *Xhosa Fireside Tales*. Phyllis Savory comments, "As with most other Bantu tales, the ones in this collection are constructed so that part of one tale can be interchanged with and fitted into another, forming a new tale. As can be imagined, the expansion in this manner is endless." In this story, one may guess that some details from the story of Aladdin have been incorporated into the Xhosa tale.